Monsieur Singh's Loves and Losses

Born and brought up in India, Sherarat E Singh makes his home in the Loire Valley in France. He teaches English, performs jazz poetry and collects vintage paperbacks.

Monsieur Singh's Loves and Losses

SHERARAT E SINGH

HarperCollins *Publishers* India

First published in India in 2013 by
HarperCollins *Publishers* India

Building 10, Tower A, 4th Floor, DLF Cyber City, Phase II,
Gurugram Haryana – 122002, India
www.harpercollins.co.in

ISBN: 978-93-5029-717-9

2 4 6 8 10 9 7 5 3 1

Typeset in 10.5/13.3 Sabon
Saanvi Graphics Noida
Printed and bound at
MicroPrints India, New Delhi

To the spirit of losers who fight and fail.

To mama, without whom I wouldn't fly.
To Emilie, without whom I wouldn't make it this far.
To mom and dad, who did what they could.

Prologue

As a rule, all educated Indians who go abroad make a killing. They make it big in business or have high-flying jobs, they bring home the booty, spread it at their parents' feet and make them proud. Even the uneducated ones own several restaurants. Yours truly, mesdames et messieurs, is an exception to the rule. 'Singh is King' is definitely not me. The entire decade of my expat life has yielded... nothing. Zéro. I used to think I was a go-getter. But that was just a lie. I ain't nothin' but a loser, crying all the time. All my friends and enemies from school and college have successful careers, houses, cars. Even children. My cousins who were kids when I left home are now grown up and enjoying successful careers – as an engineer, a chef, a dentist, a merchant navy man. They are at least ten years ahead of me, both professionally and socially. And where am I? I'm a dead duck, in the rut I'm stuck.

Do you ever feel that way? Like you're stagnating, and you don't know how to get yourself out? I mean, you can dig the difficulty of my situation only if you've been there yourself. Just like you can dig what it's like to have a bosomy brunette at the end of one's cock only if the cock happens to be your own. Right now I'm sitting here wondering how a hip guy like me got so fucked up. How come I got nowhere? And how do I stir myself out of stagnation and take it to the next level?

1

I'll start with a quick rundown on my lousy childhood, loveless teens and all that David Copperfield kinda crap. I was born in a pretty fucked up backward cow-town called Masti in Uttar Pradesh. We were a lower-middle-class Sikh family. Parents fought all the time. Then dad left home to live elsewhere in the same town, which was quite a big deal in those days. My little brother Samar and I lived with mom. We had money problems. If my mother's father hadn't given her a one-room house before he passed away, we wouldn't have a roof over our heads. Mom vented her frustration by beating me and I vented mine by torturing my brother. We were both good at school, though. And we bravely faced up to the social stigma of our parents not living together. When I completed the seventh standard at the small English-medium school in Masti, we were sent to a boarding school in Mohali, near Chandigarh. Most of my dad's side of the family lived there. I was the smallest boy my age in that school, and I know all about being bullied and wanting to cut people's balls off in their sleep. I've always been five feet four and three-fourth. People often reminded me how small I was. That's a typical Indian thing, isn't it, telling people what's wrong with them? You're too short, your hair is falling, your nose is too long, your clothes don't match, your wife is fat. When I finished high school, I wanted to be a fashion designer. Not many people knew what that meant at that time. I have always been hip that way, always into something beyond the grasp of the hoi-polloi. I spent hours drawing men's jackets and trousers, reading magazines and newspapers and cutting out pictures of interestingly dressed people. My idol was the handsome Rohit Khosla, India's first fashion designer. He'd passed away a few years ago. I wanted to study at NIFT. All the top Indian designers came from there. You had to be a graduate to enter NIFT, so I enrolled for a BA in DAV College. Three years down the drain.

Those years are mixed up in my mind. It's a hodgepodge of college, Alliance Française, a girl called Mani Walia, Webster's dictionary, MBA exams and a whole lotta boredom. I was basically a lonely teenager with eccentric ways. My music was Elvis, The Doors, The Rolling Stones, Led Zep and blues and jazz. My heroes were Dev Anand and Humphrey Bogart. The Indian press said Dev Anand imitated Gregory Peck, but I knew if he ever imitated anybody, it was Cary Grant.

I had a few friends but we didn't really have fun together. There wasn't much fun to be had in Chandigarh, anyway. No places to go out, no cafés, no culture, no pedestrian streets. You'd expect better from an entire city built by the great Le Corbusier.

I wouldn't have minded a girlfriend, but had none. Life in Chandigarh was as dry as could be.

I would go to college, come back to my rented room and read Webster's *New World Dictionary*. Yes, I used to read the dictionary, like a book. I bought it for 250 rupees out of my pocket money. I spent a lot of time caressing its pages, learning new words, expressions and pronunciations. And I was stupid enough to use them on people. 'Sir, I am a Johnny-come-lately to the college, may I join your class?'

My afternoons were spent in the college library, reading and daydreaming. That's what kept me going. Khushwant Singh, Shobhaa De, Balwant Gargi. Only people in those books – the socialites and the literati – seemed to have any fun. And loads of sex. It must have been about then that I developed a penchant for the salacious.

Along with college, I also enrolled in a part-time fashion design course at a newly opened small-time institute in Chandigarh. You know, the kind that starts mushrooming to cash in on a new trend. I thought it would help me prepare for NIFT. The place was swarming with clean-shaven, snobby, rich kids who came to the institute on motorbikes and in fancy cars. I was the only one who rode in on a bicycle. And I was the only one who wore a turban, which added to my uncoolness. The boys talked about private parties and other rich-kid stuff and hooked up easily with the girls. If my daddy had the dough and I drove around in a sexy car, I'd hook up too. I was clearly out of place. Besides, the instructor – a skinny, snobby bitch – didn't teach much by way of design. Pretty soon, the cost of buying cloth and the ordeal of measuring, cutting, tailoring and being a poor unsexy kid got to me. I started missing classes and finally decided never to go back. The experience put me off fashion design as a career choice. And it cost my dad 10,000 rupees that he had shelled out after a lot of pleading.

Now I needed another vent for my creative energies. No sex was in sight, so I joined French classes. *C'est la vie, je ne sais quoi, savoir faire, ménage à trois*. All those colourful French expressions that I learnt from my Webster's had made it a very attractive language to me. Alliance Française provided the stimulation I needed to be happy and I really was happy there, speaking the language of the fabled French lover. Now I went to college, to Alliance twice a week, and spent time with my Webster's. I also started using my dad's old Priya scooter which he had got repaired and repainted for me. I must have been the only guy in Chandigarh on that extinct species of two-wheeler in 1996.

The elementary three-month course at Alliance went by quickly. I attended every class religiously and saw films every Saturday – they mostly showed French classics from the sixties and seventies. Those movies were a terrific experience – cinematic, intellectual and erotic. It was a whole new world of perception. A world where bare-bosomed blondes with luscious lips looked out of the window and smiled; ladies of the French revolution lifted their long ornate dresses saying *Fais-moi l'amour;* femme fatales spread their legs and whispered *Oui oui oui oui oui*; and Jeanne Moreau wandered about in the Parisian night to the sounds of jazz. Quite a different scene from your immature Bollywood cornball. I totally dug *le cinéma française*. And I dug Alain Delon, his handsome looks, icy suave and flair for getting into any lady's pants anytime of the day.

I enrolled for the next level of French and was graced with the presence of Mani Walia. I was immediately bewitched, bothered and bewildered by her, sentimental fool that I was. She had the face of an angel, and though not endowed with a great figure, she carried herself like a princess. I loved her classy clothes and fine make-up. Most of all, I loved her repartee. She was twenty-five, I was nineteen. I was madly in love with her and wrote funny poems using words like 'paramour' and 'cicisbeo'. One night I even dreamt of her nibbling at my fingers and my underwear got wet. She didn't give me the time of day. I was heartbroken for the next two years.

I had to start preparing for the MBA entrance exams but I couldn't concentrate. Couldn't stop thinking about Mani. I was obsessed with her. I had tried to talk to her about it but she was having none of that. I even sent my friend Manish to follow her car and get me her address and then wrote her a long letter explaining my feelings. Later, I gave her a call and she banged down the phone after telling me not to call her again. I went back to Masti to see my mother and told her about my heartache. Mom took me to Delhi to meet Sharmaji, her spiritual guide.

A frail, soft-spoken man, Sharmaji taught me how to meditate: sit down in a calm place, lights off, pick an image in your mind – any image – and a name for the image. Then you bring the image to the centre of the forehead and try to superimpose the name on the image so that they are both at the centre of the forehead as one. Easier explained than done, of course, but I tried, and it really did help me be joyful again in the next few months. Come to think of it, it might have been the power of meditation that accelerated my departure. My first three years in France, I meditated regularly. Then it became less frequent due to lack of time, and now I haven't meditated in five years. Maybe that's the reason why I'm not getting anywhere.

After my disenchantment with fashion design, my next career choice was advertising. I thought I was good at the English language and I was fascinated by the prospect of making a living by coming up with clever slogans and ad copy, *Mad Men* style. After the BA final year exams, I worked as trainee copywriter in a small ad agency. A successful young copywriter at the agency said I had good taste and a fine mind. I loved that compliment. A fine mind! Along with the ad agency job, I wasted many more months preparing, taking and failing various competitive exams, including NIFT. I just wasn't good enough. Finally I went to Bombay in search of jobs with bigger advertising agencies.

I'd directly go to the agency offices and try to see the creative director, without much luck. While in Bombay, I auditioned for the All India Radio. I thought it would be pretty cool to rock the city with the blues. Of course, they didn't pick me up, the philistines.

I was crashing with an acquaintance from Masti who lived in the suburbs of Bombay. One room, mattress-on-the-floor, stove-in-the-corner kind of situation. Catching the local train from the suburbs to the city every day made me realize that even with a copywriting job in Bombay, my life would be like the passengers of that train – go to work each day in an overcrowded train, sweating all the way in the clammy, maritime heat. Come back home, dead tired, and doze off with an open mouth amidst the stench of sweat and god knows what else. It was like the setting of a Milan Kundera novel. That straphanging life was never going to make me happy. And I doubted if I'd ever get laid living in those conditions. I had to find a way out. I had to get away.

A guy I met at the Alliance Française in Bombay brought to my attention a master's degree programme at a tourism school in France. The course was taught in English and the fees were not too high. Up to that point, the idea of going abroad had been a vague, distant dream, but now I was pretty sure that if I stayed in India, something bad would happen to me. I had to break through to the other side. Not that my parents had the resources, but I had to try. I quickly filled out the admission application for the tourism school in Angers, applied for a grant at the French embassy in New Delhi, and went to meet the university's agent in Hyderabad. Dad outright refused to fork out any money, his usual stance when it came to doing anything different. Mom said she would get the money. Finally it was mama, my mother's brother, who owned a cinema and other businesses in Masti, who came to the rescue.

After a lot of talking to many different people, collecting information, months of desperation, aggravation, paperwork, spending money and running around, I finally boarded the plane to Paris.

2

The flight was okay. I sat next to a pleasant, tall and skinny, blond, blue-eyed German girl. She was nice to talk to and said that the girls in France were going to like me, with my exotic looks and all. I landed at Charles de Gaulle Airport at dawn. I was wearing the grey blazer that had been part of Samar's school uniform, green corduroys and my trademark little black turban. After a tumultuous relationship with the standard turban, I had devised my own personal style. It went around the head three times instead of six. It was lighter and in harmony with my extra-small size.

'*Passporr*,' growled the intimidating immigration officer in her thick African voice. '*Passporr*.' She had to growl twice before I understood what she wanted. The baggage claim was huge and crowded. After I got my luggage, I went to the TGV station, bought a ticket for Angers, and stared at the arrivals and departures in confusion for the next half hour. Then I gave up and asked somebody in broken French which train to board.

It was cold as hell on the platform and my balls almost froze. On the train, I carried my cumbersome luggage through the aisle to my seat. 'You can put your bags over there, in the back,' said a kind gentleman in French. I realized there was space for luggage just by the door. After taking the bags one by one back where they belonged, I asked the gentleman if I could sit next to him. He said yes, and we got talking. His name was Gilles Garza and he was some sort of mechanic at a company in Angers that made aeroplane parts. He looked like he was in his early forties but was actually much older, as I learnt later. He gave me survival tips on French culture. We passed snow along the way and Gilles said it rarely snowed in Angers. When we arrived, Gilles hailed a cab and gave me a ride to my school, ESTHUA, at 41 Place Imbach, where they have the Museum of Natural History today. He gave me his phone number before saying goodbye.

The foreign students' in-charge drove me to Centre Diocésain and got me a room. The huge eighteenth-century diocese served as a hostel for students and travellers. At the main entrance of the building was a plaque that told visitors never to forget that more than 800 Jews had been detained there before being sent to concentration camps in 1942 and 1943. I liked the room. It was a tiny rectangle with wooden floors, a small bed, a cupboard, a sink and a large window. A smaller but brighter version of Alain Delon's room in *Le Samouraï*. There was a common shower on the same floor. The rent was almost twice what I had been promised but the cheaper rooms were not yet available.

I opened the window and inhaled the winter air. Whatever the rent, for now I was glad just to be in France, the land of clean air, snow, beautiful women and freedom.

For the first few days, I walked around the streets saying *bonjour* to everybody I passed. I didn't know then that you don't greet strangers on the street, even in France. I met the other Indian students who were going to be in my class. I was utterly disappointed – I had been told by Shahrukh Salaam, the university agent, that I would be studying in a multi-cultural environment with French, Australian and American students. That was the whole point of my leaving India. And here I was, stuck with exactly the kind of people I was trying to get away from. Most of them were from Hyderabad, for the simple reason that Shahrukh fucking Salaam lived there. Those guys moved together in a herd, lived next to each other in the students' hostel, and were always censuring anything I did or said. They were an exaggerated form of all that I hated about India.

There were only two things I hated about Angers: the excess of dog shit on the pavements and the Indian guys. I tried to avoid both. Nevertheless, there were two Indian guys I did like. One was a small, round, funny, good-hearted fella from Hyderabad. The other was this quiet, plain-looking guy from Bangalore who went by the name of Prabhakar. I found out much later that Prabhakar was penetrating a girl from the *guide-interprète* class. She had a great ass. I think he also balled the French slut who had a thing for Indian dick. And he never once boasted about anything to anybody. Sort of a quiet maverick, a real chhupa rustam.

Classes wouldn't start until the last week of January so I spent my first three weeks in Angers taking in the razzle-dazzle of my new world. I was like Alice in Wonderland. I was taken by the cobbled pedestrian streets and mystified by the long city buses that snaked through the narrow streets without colliding into anything. Chateau d'Angers with its seventeen watch towers was enthralling. It stood by the river, right in the middle of Angers, like a massive, seventeen-limb stone octopus guarding the city.

There were life-sized pictures of scantily clad ladies in lingerie shop windows, shoes that were splendidly designed and made of the finest leather, the people were courteous and the girls were beautiful, with charming smiles and sumptuous behinds.

I thought I had died and gone to heaven. The women were like none I had ever seen. They had slender waists that ended in smooth wide hips, a back that arched so perfectly it made you want to slide down the curve and fall into the deep dark crevice below and never come up. They were like walking sculptures that until now I had seen only in movies and magazines. And the clothes they wore... ooh la la! The clinging tops, flowing skirts, tights, stretch jeans, high boots, low necklines... oh god! It was Fashion TV in the flesh.

I was overwhelmed, I didn't know if I wanted to fuck them all or just sit and watch them move forever. The sheer abundance of women in Angers was overwhelming. I could feast my eyes on any street in the city. I had never experienced that in India. Not in Chandigarh, not in Delhi, nor in Bombay. And statistically, they had three women to one man in France. It was heaven. In France, you can make out the tantalizing fullness of a woman's posterior even through a winter coat. Panties peeking out of pants is a common sight. The butt-crack is visible more often than not, which I consider vulgar, but the sight of it did send a trickle of thrill down there. How I loved to watch those asses move and sway and stay still and sit down and stand up...

I was meant to live in this country. I was like *l'Homme qui Aimait les Femmes*, always turning around for booty observation. I would change direction for the pleasure of walking behind a delectable derrière. I would pretend to look at shop windows while ass-watching from the corner of the eye. I am a derrière-devil, baby. The female ass holds for me never-ending fascination. You know, like an art lover who goes into a museum and gazes at a painting for hours. I was equally thrilled to discover that it was normal for people to kiss in public places. And I don't mean a quick peck on the cheek, but a solid kiss on the mouth.

On street corners and sidewalk benches you will find teenage lovers locked in each other's arms. It was exactly the kind of freedom of expression I had been yearning for all my adolescent life. In India, even holding hands in public raised eyebrows. I wished I had been born here. I wandered the pedestrian streets, checking out shop windows and women, never going into cafés for fear of spending money and not knowing what to drink. I spent a lot of time at the university libraries in St Serge and Place Imbach, browsing books and babes. One evening, I was sitting across a cute girl with long, reddish-blond, curly hair and freckles, and I spent an hour planning in my head how to ask her out for a drink. But I didn't have the balls, and had to go back to my room all alone. It was a long walk. And in the dead of the night the Centre Diocésain building looked like a haunted palace out of a scary movie. One Saturday morning, while checking out the flea market at Place Imbach, I ran into Gilles Garza, the guy from the train. He took me to a café at Place du Ralliement, the main square in Angers, and bought me my first glass of rosé. I told him I felt lonely, I didn't have friends. He said it was difficult to make friends in France and said I could call him if I needed anything. What I needed was a little French miss to practise the legendary French kiss, and to teach me how to eat. I mean food, how to eat food. In the first two weeks in Angers, I didn't know what to eat and where. I went down to the dining hall of Centre Diocésain one evening but found the potato purée and steak disgusting. Thankfully, the breakfast there was meant for human consumption: tea, coffee, bread, butter, jam. For lunch and dinner I was sustained by a packet of madeleines. Then I found out I could eat at the university restaurant at St Serge. The food was good and relatively cheap. The first day, I had roast chicken and fries; next I tried out a pizza that looked really yummy with thick pieces of grilled meat. First bite and I wanted to puke. What I took for meat was some kind of seafood. That was the first and last time I ever tried anything coming out of the sea.

One Sunday, I bought a *pain au chocolat* in a boulangerie and thought the French were strange to put chocolate inside bread. Lo and behold, it was love at first bite.

It was in my second week at Centre Diocésain that I met Marie. She sat next to me at the breakfast table. Marie had rented a room there. She was very kind. I told her I was lonely and she lent me her CD player and a CD of jazz oldies. On Sunday, she brought me brioche from church. I asked her out for a drink and she dilly-dallied but invited me to have dinner in her room the following evening. I took a little bottle of *vin de table* Pays d'Hérault, bought at LIDL. LIDL is the cheapest supermarket in Europe – students, alcoholics, foreigners and poor people shop there – and Pays d'Hérault is the cheapest, most vulgar wine there can be. But I didn't know any better.

Marie's room was bigger than mine and included a little kitchenette. She said she didn't drink wine. We ate chicken and rice. I had a little wine and felt tipsy by the end of the meal. Don't recall the conversation. She was a psychology student at the Catholic University and was always busy with studies and projects, so we never went out for a drink or anything. I got the feeling that she was not the type of girl who went out for drinks. Later I realized she was what the French call *Catho*, meaning somebody who is a devout

Catholic, goes to church on Sunday, dresses in a classic, rather bland manner, concentrates on studies and career and doesn't go out, or goes only with Catholic friends.

I wished I had met a girl who'd take me to her room and fuck my brains out. That's one of my zillion unmaterialized fantasies, to fuck a stranger in a room at Centre Diocésain. I saw Marie from time to time over the next year and a half before losing touch. She was always nice and encouraging and even fed me late one evening when I dropped by unannounced.

The Indian guys spent a lot of time in the computer room at ESTHUA, often entire days, which was somewhat unnerving for the French guys who wanted to use the computer but couldn't because the Indian guys wouldn't budge. I spent some time there as well, and learnt that using a computer was about more than just emailing. I hadn't had much to do with computers back home. One day in the computer room, it must have been the third week of January, I saw this girl who I thought was magnificent. She was tall with pale, flawless skin, luscious bow-shaped lips, sea-blue eyes, auburn hair... a princess out of a fairytale. I had already seen her around the premises. As I stood up to leave, I went up to her casually and said, '*Bonjour, comment vous appelez-vous?*' Hello, what's your name?

'Jennifer,' she said, looking apprehensive.

'I think all French girls are beautiful but you're the most beautiful.'

'*Merci*,' she said with only a hint of a smile.

A few days later, I was in the ESTHUA library, which was housed in a typical *Angevine* style building with waxed wooden floors, large windows and square wooden tables – a lovely place to sit and ruminate on a sunny day in winter. I was browsing through the books on the shelves when I came face to face with *la plus belle* Jennifer.

'Bonjour, ça va?' she said.

'Bonjour. I'm fine.'

'Where are you from?'

'India.'

'Oh, I'd love to go to India. How are you faring in France? Do you need any help?'

'I'm doing okay, thanks,' I replied. 'Hey, actually, could you help me make a CV in French?'

She agreed and we went to a nearby café. That was my first ever coffee with a French girl in France, and what a girl. We talked a little, she asked questions about India and my family, told me she was from Nantes. Then she had to leave. She paid for coffee, spread her wings and flew away.

I went to the library again the following afternoon, but she wasn't there. The next day I tried the computer room but missed her again. A day or two later she reappeared in the library, in the same fashion as she had the first time. She gave me a copy of her CV and told me to make mine on the same lines. She also said that she was soon going to do an internship on a cruise boat. Then she disappeared again, for a longer period this time. I was desperate to see her. I spotted her again weeks later, but she seemed to be in a hurry and said she was leaving for the cruise next week. I never saw her again.

A few years ago, I came across her CV among my papers from that time, and called the number on it. Her mother gave me her email. I emailed and she replied, but only vaguely remembered me, if at all. She asked me what I was up to. I told her I taught English and was married, and that it would be nice to get together in Nantes or Angers. I never heard back from her. This happens to me all the time. Every time I tell a woman I'm married, she loses interest. What happened to all the open-minded broads who used to lust after married men?

Last week of January. Classes started. I felt a little more familiar with my surroundings now. My class was an interesting mix of different cultures – apart from the Indian students, there were Chinese, Americans and Australians. Everyone tended to hang out with their own kind. The Chinese students never turned off this cell phones in class, and always rushed out when they got a call.

I got friendly with Jeffrey, a student from Florida, when we sat next to each other during a school trip. Naturally, we got to talking about women. Jeffrey was with a different girl every other day, and he gave me some tips on how to seduce French women.

'Getting any?' I would often ask him as a form of greeting.

'Not since last night.'

He also gave me tips on improving my American diction. I taught him to say *bhenchod*, which got him in trouble with the Indian guys.

'Shoot that shit, man,' he would say.

Here's a funny story about Jeffrey. On a school trip to Paris, we were put up in a youth hostel with bunk beds and common toilets, near the Mastille. The first night, all the students went out in their usual groups. I tagged along with a group of French students from the *guide-interprète* programme. The next morning, as I came out of the loo, I was witness to an unforgettable sight. There was Jeffrey squatting on the floor, drooling like a retard, a thick streak of piss between his legs making its way towards me and under him a huge turd that had freshly exited his bowels. Surprisingly, it didn't stink. Jeffrey looked at me with glazed eyes and made a grimace of relief. I ran out, shocked.

After breakfast, one of the teachers told us that somebody had left the toilets in a disgusting state and that we ought to drink responsibly. A little later, I ran into Jeffrey, who had recovered by now, and he raised an embarrassed finger to his lips. I never betrayed him. Until now, that is.

A month later, I found a cheaper room at a youth hostel near Foyer des Jeunes Travailleurs at the Belle-Beille campus. Around the same time, I met Krystyna in the university library. One afternoon, I was just sitting there lost in existential reflection on the burning issue of how to get laid when I spotted this exotic-looking girl with straight red hair. I gathered my balls, approached her and asked her the meaning of a French word.

'I'll look up the dictionary,' she said with a shy smile.

'You don't know what it means?' I said in surprise.

'I'm not French.'

'So, what are you?'

'I'm Hungarian.'

Hungarian! Wow. I was thrilled at the opportunity of meeting not only the French but also other Europeans in France. I was on the crossroads of cultures. I had never thought about Hungary in any way, except maybe while reading a Jeffrey Archer novel. So we got talking. Krystyna was doing a *licence* in tourism development. Licence is a three-year graduate degree. Then on, I often ran into her at the library with two French girls. The three were writing a project together. I liked the quiet brunette with the old-fashioned name, Gisèle.

The next time I found Krystyna alone, we talked about our lives and I asked her out for a drink but she said she had other plans. Two weeks after we first met, I paid her a surprise visit at the university hostel with a bar of chocolate and suggested we go out for a drink. She took the chocolate but said she was meeting a friend that evening.

'Okay, another time,' I said. She nodded and seemed to be in a hurry for me to go. So I left, feeling disappointed and lonely. The next day, I was in a telephone booth at Ralliement. It was dark, the shops had closed and the street lights had come on. I spotted Krystyna coming from the opposite direction, hand in hand with a tall guy. I was so surprised I stared at them through the glass, just to make sure it was her. It was her all right. She caught my gaze. I managed a limp wave of my hand and began fiddling with the dial. So this was why she wouldn't go out with me – she was already going out with the tall guy. But I couldn't understand why she didn't tell me she was seeing somebody else. It would have saved me some time and embarrassment. The time I wasted thinking about her could have been used to find love elsewhere.

A year later, I came across the tall boyfriend and we became friends. I asked him if he knew why Krystyna had kept me in the dark. Léo explained that Krystyna was the kind of girl who needed to have people interested in her all the time. Besides, she liked me. Had she told me she was going out with someone, I might not have been as interested in her. Treachery, thy name is woman.

I still had no real friends to speak of but I had kept in touch with Gilles Garza since our last meeting at the flea market almost a month ago. I called him every now and then to say hello and to tell him how I was faring in Angers. Gilles was always kind and encouraging and he certainly picked up on my loneliness. One late afternoon in February, I was in my room at the hostel and had just finished eating brioche stuffed with canned tuna. I hadn't learnt to hate tuna yet, and didn't know that brioche was eaten for breakfast. There was a knock. I answered the door, and a dandily dressed Gilles said, 'Let's go, we're going to have some fun.' I was taken by surprise. And delight. There was somebody in this foreign land who wanted to take me some place to have some fun.

Gilles took me to a friend's place for aperitif. They were a cute couple and asked me a lot of questions about India, and what I thought of France. Then we went to a pizzeria, Gilles and I. He introduced me to the lady who owned the place. Gilles always introduced me to people as if I were some special person come from far away.

'You know, ze woman and I, we were togezer,' Gilles told me with a wink.

After a delicious pizza quatre-nichons, we went to a discotheque, Le Bolero, opposite 400 Coups cinema. Gilles danced and I sat sulking on a sofa by myself until he dragged me to the dance floor. Gilles took off his shirt and danced as if in a trance. He had an excellent physique for a man his age. I picked up some courage and danced alone to the beats of '*Tomber la chemise*'. Gilles introduced me to some people he didn't know. I tried to pick up a girl, but failed as usual. We went back to Gilles's place with a forty-year-old woman accompanied by a much younger man. He was okay to look at and she was not good-looking at all. I didn't understand how or why they ended up in Gilles's apartment. We talked until three in the morning, then the couple left and Gilles drove me back to the youth hostel. That was my first 'fun' outing in Angers. Uneventful but interesting.

After that, I called Gilles often. He would pick me up and take me out for drinks or dinner. We would talk about life, love and ladies. He paid every time. It's impossible to find a friend like that in France today.

Every Friday, our class took a trip to a nearby city with the French students from the *guide-interprète* programme who were preparing to be multi-lingual tour guides. There were twenty of them, mostly girls. It gave me a chance to actually speak and improve my French. Thanks to these class trips, I got to see many French cities that I would never have visited otherwise. We visited Le Mans, Tours, Paris, Versailles, Deauville, Honfleur... We explored so many chateaux, churches and cathedrals that soon I was indifferent to the architecture and beauty of these monuments. We visited the Menhirs of Carnac, which I had read about in *101 Mysteries of the World*, the American cemetery in Normandy where Jeffrey's grandfather was buried, and the D-day beaches. Until now World War II had been just a chapter in history books for me, but here I realized how important it was in the history and lives of the French and other Europeans. It was part of their general consciousness.

And of course we went wine tasting in the vineyards around Angers. Anjou – the historical name of the Angers area – is famous for its high quality wines, especially the sweet white wines Coteaux du Layon and Coteaux de l'Aubance. I can't stand these, too sweet for my taste. Our teacher taught us how to taste wine: tilt the glass, observe the colour of the wine, swirl it in the glass, sniff it, take a sip, don't swallow, inhale some air through the mouth, feel the flavour, spit it out, take another sip. Prabhakar didn't take the spitting out seriously and got slightly drunk.

I was like an excited nut on these trips, talking to everybody and laughing all the time. They often asked me what kept me so happy. Well, the joy I felt on Fridays came from being able to practise my French with all those beautiful people. I was living my dream. I was the only foreign student who spoke proper French. It was fun cracking Indian-style jokes in French.

'Show me your palm and I'll look into your future.'

'Ah, oui!' said Ludivine, extending her palm.

'I see that you are going to have two beautiful children.'

'Ah, oui?'

'Oui. One of them is going to look like you and the other will look like me,' I said, cracking up.

'I don't want to have children with you,' said Ludivine with a whack on my head. Everyone around us laughed. We could have made a fun couple, Ludivine and I. Alas, neither Ludivine nor any of the other guides offered me a visit to the sacred chapel between their legs. Real life is nothing like films and books where the white lady leads the brown boy into a corner and places his hand on her bosom.

Looking back, I understand why I didn't get laid. Simply because I was not initiated in the ways of the world. I had turned myself into a curiosity. I was the jolly Indian guy who spoke French and laughed all the time. Everybody knew me but I wasn't really close to anyone. I've learnt that people don't take you seriously if you laugh all the time, especially if you're a man.

Women think you're weird if you're always joking around. I was like the laughing Buddha that everybody liked but none imagined fucking. I myself was mostly thinking of being with them, not within. I gave out no sex vibes. I had no focus, I wanted to be with all of them and speak French. And I spoke too much. Too fucking much to connect with a single girl on an emotional or sexual level. I was too dazed by the sight of those gorgeous girls to be a subtle sex machine.

Worse, I became infatuated with one of the guides on the Paris trip. It started like it always does – repartee, friendship, flirtation, infatuation. Clémence had long blond hair and was utterly charming. I felt an emotional connection with her; fool that I was, I'd feel an emotional connection with anyone in those days. She laughed at my jokes, taught me new French expressions, and was always warm towards me. What really did it for me was the way she sang '*Je ne veux pas travailler*'. That song never fails to bring back the heartaches of that first year in France.

On the last Friday of February, after a trip to Tours, the bus dropped us off at Place Imbach, the usual pick-up and drop-off point, and I walked Clémence home. At her door, I told her I had fallen for her. She was gracious about it and said she already had a boyfriend, a policeman. Besides, she didn't want to go to India to live with me. Who said I was going back to India? Anyway, that was that, and once again I checked into heartbreak hotel. Big time. On the next class trip, I didn't talk much and quietly read *Memory Babe*, a biography of Jack Kerouac that I had stumbled upon in the library. Clémence noticed my moodiness and kept her distance.

Sunday was the most boring day of the week – no classes, no libraries, no shops open, and all the students went away for the weekend. Angers looked like a ghost town. The Sunday after my confession to Clémence I got really blue, so I called Gilles. When he came over to see me and asked what had happened, I said I was so embarrassed I didn't know where to begin.

'She pregnant?'

'Of course not.' I felt even more embarrassed that Gilles was thinking too highly of me. To get a girl pregnant, you had to stick your dick into her, but I hadn't even come close to holding her hand. I explained, and Gilles took me on a drive and said wise things, the kind an experienced, older man will say to a callow youth about matters of the heart.

I saw Clémence again about a week later, and asked her to help me with my French CV. She came down to my hostel the following evening just for that – she was probably thankful that I was no longer sulking at her. That evening, I spoke to her at length about my feelings, and gave her a poem I had written. It was the last time I had a proper conversation with her. Our later meetings were just *salut* and *au revoir*. I was cleansed of strong feelings for Clémence but still there were days when I thought about her and felt blue. At the obligatory medical examination, the doctor asked if I had any ailments I knew of. I said, 'Yeah, heartache.'

I left the room at the youth hostel and, at Prabhakar's suggestion, moved into his tiny room in the students' hostel. The deal was that I would chip in with half the rent, 250 francs. Two in one room were not allowed and if found out, Prabhakar would be expelled. But that sharp little bastard wasn't afraid to take risks to save a few hundred francs. I admired his guts. I wouldn't have the balls to do that if it were my room. I slept on the floor and went in and out through the window. It was inconvenient but adventurous.

A week later, out of the blue, I thought of Clémence and felt miserable again. I wanted to call Gilles but it was early afternoon and he would be at work, so I called Francis. Francis was this tall, good-looking, blue-eyed dude I had met in the computer room at ESTHUA. A very nice guy with a broad smile. Francis and I decided to meet at the library. I arrived fifteen minutes early, and spotted Gisèle, the quiet brunette friend of Krystyna's. She was sitting by herself. I went up to her and said, 'Hello, do you mind if I sit here?' She didn't mind. We made small talk until Francis arrived and suggested we go to a café. Now originally it was supposed to be just Francis and me, because I wanted to talk to him about Clémence. But I couldn't resist the impulse to ask Gisèle to join us. She hesitated for a second and said yes.

The cure of fuckstration is to have another lead in sight. Though I wasn't exactly building any hopes about Gisèle, her presence in the café was like the balm of Gilead on my aching heart. After half an hour of inconsequential conversation, Francis left. Gisèle and I were in no hurry. We continued to talk – about music, food, where our families were from, that sort of stuff. The music in the café was nice and low, brassy jazz and funk. And all of a sudden, it was Ray Charles raving, 'I got a woman...'

'That's my song!' I exclaimed, half-jumping out of the couch. Gisèle, after her initial surprise, laughed for the first time, revealing perfect teeth. It was restrained laughter but her eyes lit up. The song was a straw in the wind, it heralded what was to come. We talked for another hour, then I asked if she wanted to leave – not that I wanted to leave, not that I had anything better to do, but I didn't want to appear clingy. She said okay, and we left. I shook her hand as we said goodbye. Oh yes, it was early days yet and I was still shaking hands with girls instead of kissing them on the cheek. It was a weird resistance on my part not to do as the French do. I shook hands with pretty babes when they offered me their cheek for a kiss.

Two days later, I ran into Gisèle in the library. I did not suggest going for a drink, though I was dying for some company and someone to spill my heart out to and tell them how sad and lonely I felt and that I needed someone to love. But I didn't think I had the courage to have that conversation with Gisèle. I ran into her again a few days later. I was in a brighter mood this time and asked her out for a drink We went to Bar du Centre. We talked. Rather, I talked and she sat back, looking dreamy-eyed and mysterious. Smoke from her cigarette filled the space between us and she reminded me of Uma Thurman in the *Pulp Fiction* poster. I loved looking at her. Only three months earlier I had been shambling through the squalor of life in India, desperately searching for a way out, and now here I was sitting in a typical French café that had probably not been refurbished since the seventies, gazing at a gorgeous belle of vintage looks.

Then I didn't see her any more. It could have been the holidays – too many holidays in this country – or simply that we did not have classes in the same building, or perhaps she had been too busy to go to the library. I didn't have her phone number. I hadn't asked and she hadn't volunteered the information. After a week I ran into her again somewhere, and we went to Bar du Centre. We talked, she smoked and sipped at her drink and I gazed into her eyes.

So this was how it went for more than two months. We'd run into each other by chance and go for a drink, then there would be a long absence before we met again. Once, she took me to her apartment and introduced me to her younger sister, Hélène. Gisèle didn't talk much and we never got very close or very friendly; it was a strange sort of friendship. I liked her, but never fantasized about her. I was unable to express my feelings for her.

That spring, I moved to the students' residence, Cuffon Pavot. It was a mixed residence where boys and girls had rooms side by side, providing a great opportunity for cross-gender friendships. My room was on the second floor, and there were only two guys on that floor – me and Tim, an Australian student. The girls there came to know of me as the Indian student who didn't shave and sang 'Love Me Tender' in the shower.

Two or three weeks into my stay there, I ran into this cute girl on my floor. I had seen her around. She had delicate white skin and pale blond curly hair. I was having trouble with the vending machine and she happened to be passing by. I asked her if she knew how to get back my money which the machine had just swallowed. She said I should ask the concierge.

'Thank you. What's your name?'

'Céline.' She said we were neighbours on the second floor and I could knock on her door if I wanted to have coffee with her sometime. Not one to miss an opportunity, I said, 'Let's go out tomorrow.' So the next evening, she drove us to the city centre in her red car. We chatted and drank beer. I hadn't yet developed a dislike for beer, and used to take it with a twist of lime. She said she loved the smells when I cooked in the common kitchen, and it made her laugh when she heard me singing in the shower. I paid for the drinks and she looked at me as if I were a prince. We took a stroll around Ralliement. I had no idea how she felt about me or where this was going. Or maybe I knew, but just didn't know how to handle the situation. I had no plan of action. So I did nothing. In retrospect, I realize I was so afraid of being rejected that I did not let myself build any hopes about her. I was too overcome with negativity to take any positive action. So I feigned a sort of distance that did not allow the transition from first base to the second. It was like when you need something real bad and it's offered to you on a platter, it seems too good to be true. You're afraid to reach out and grab it 'coz you believe it to be an illusion. You don't go the distance because you're afraid to die chasing the mirage.

We drove back to the hostel.

'Would you like some coffee?' Céline offered when we were outside her room. So we had coffee and made small talk. When I ran out of things to say, I said it was late and I should go. She nodded.

'Thank you for the coffee,' I said as I stood up.

'My pleasure,' she said with a winsome smile.

I hesitated. 'Ah... um...'

'Yes?' she said eagerly, inching closer, her eyes expectant, her chin turned up. The distance between us was minimal. All I had to do was bend forward, place my hands on her waist and kiss her lips. But fear of rejection got me by the balls. I just looked at her.

'Goodnight,' I managed to say before I rushed out of the door. I don't recall if I felt bad about it that night, but I do now. She wanted me, she had made that abundantly clear. But I was a dumb fool and let that opportunity on a platter just sit there and be wasted. It's what I call POPS, the pussy-on-a-platter syndrome: the extreme slowing or complete numbing of the sexual instinct when the opportunity to have sex is right in front of you. I kick myself every time I'm reminded of Céline. I see her standing there in a black dress, eyes half closed, her mouth ready to receive mine.

The next morning I slipped a note under her door saying something kitsch like 'Thank you for a lovely evening'. I did that because, first, I thought I owed it to her, and second, the note would show that I cared for her, and make her want to see me again. Well, that's the lamest fucking thing to do in a situation like this. It just goes to further prove that you're a pussy and makes sure you never get into Céline's.

I didn't see her for days. The hostel was like an apartment building, where you don't necessarily run into your neighbours every day. Then I knocked on her door one afternoon.

'Come in, come in, have a drink!' she exclaimed. She was with her best friend, and they were in a lively mood.

'We are going to a party this evening. Would you like to come?' Celine asked. 'It's going to be crazy – lots of dancing and drinking.'

'Sure,' I replied. I wasn't doing anything else and this seemed like the perfect chance to make a proper move.

A few hours later, I made my way to l'Okapi, the bar where I was supposed to meet Céline and her friend before we went to the party. On the way, I ran into some students from the guide class who I was friendly with. They were going to Rieg's place for a drink and asked me to join them. In a flash, I forgot about Céline and her party and went with them. We talked and had a drink, somebody smoked weed.

I saw Céline the next day, or the day after, and apologized.

'It does not matter,' she said, obviously disappointed.

Now, how dumb can you get? The Lord gave me a second chance to rectify my mistake and I blew it again. I'm not sure what happened, why I did not go to the party, but I think it had something to do with the description that Céline and her friend gave me, that it was a wild party and everybody would drink and dance. It could be that I was intimidated by the prospect of dancing, but mostly I think I feared that Céline might meet somebody more to her liking and spend the party making out with him, and I would be left sulking in a corner by myself. Because that was what my life was about: losing and sulking. I had no self-confidence at all, and negativity ruled my mind. Clémence's rejection had left its mark. I saw Céline one more time, when I made her some dal-chawal in the shared kitchen. I was sulky through the meal, feeling bad about not getting laid. 'You're such a serious guy,' she told me.

Then there were holidays and we lost touch. Frankly, even I wouldn't stay in touch with the guy I was back then.

3

It was the end of May and I was taking a stroll in the city one afternoon when I met Gisèle again. I found out that she was going to her parents' house for two weeks to prepare for exams. They lived in a small town near Le Mans. 'I'll see you tonight,' I told her. I went back to the hostel, took a long nap, had dinner, and was at her door at about 10:30 p.m. When I went up the stairs to the second floor, her apartment door was ajar and I was just in time to catch a glimpse of a black bra before it disappeared under her maroon shirt. I hadn't seen much of her skin before this, never saw her in a skirt, and her panties never peeked out. So seeing a bit of her bra was arousing. As I pushed open the door, her eyes said, 'Ah, you finally came, I've been longing to see you all evening!' Her mouth merely said, 'I thought you were not coming.'

I apologized for the delay. We sat down at the low metal table and talked the usual slow talk, without saying much, looking into each other's eyes, sipping tea. The maroon top clung to her like second skin and made her breasts look full and tempting. Just like the apple Adam bit into.

We were sitting at right angles and I spotted a scar on the left side of her forehead.

'What is that?' I asked.

'A cyst.'

I touched it. That was the first time I touched her. I caressed the scar and let my finger linger over it. She blushed.

'Did I ever tell you how beautiful you are?' I asked.

'*Non.*'

'I'm telling you now.'

'*Merci,*' she said and blushed again.

I got up to leave. Time for the goodbye kiss at the door. In Angers, they kiss four times, two on each cheek. Male gives, female receives. Normally it's a quick movement, the lips move from the right cheek to the left, back to the right and again the left. But that night it happened in slow motion. My lips were heavy with passion and I had a hard time going from one cheek to the other without stopping in the middle. She threw her head back before my lips could reach hers.

'I have someone!'

'Too late,' I said, and pressed my mouth on hers. She responded with eagerness. That, folks, was the most exhilarating kiss of my life, the most passionate, the most tender. For the first time in my life I was kissing someone I was in love with. For the first time I was not a loser. I was fucking Napoleon!

We stood in a loose embrace, me saying '*Je t'aime, je t'aime*', my hands roaming all over her back, sliding inside her pants to caress her beautiful, perfect ass, just feeling the roundness of it.

'You have roving hands,' she said with an impish smile.

'Why don't we lie down in bed?' I suggested.

'No.' She shook her head.

'Come on...' I took her by the hand and led her to the bed. She resisted only for a moment before following me.

I laid her down gently and kissed her all over, my hands exploring all they could, taking in the sensuousness of that fabulous body. Her body responded to my touch, but she pushed my hand away after a while.

'I love my boyfriend,' she explained. 'And he loves me too, though he doesn't show it often.'

I felt sad for her.

'I am sorry I didn't tell you about him before,' she said. 'I thought you would not be interested in being friends with me if you knew.'

Good thinking. Had I known the truth sooner, I wouldn't have dared kiss her. She said I was handsome and charming. Where else would a girl like her say that to a hairy dick like me? Certainly not in India. I wanted to take off her top. She resisted. I insisted. She gave in. The bra came off too and I found myself staring at the most gorgeous pair of bare breasts. I couldn't believe my good fortune for a minute. I tasted them, devoured them with my lips and tongue and then proceeded to relieve her of her trousers.

'No,' she whispered and this time she didn't give in. So we lay there all night, caressing and kissing, taking in all we could of each other. At about six in the morning, she made me leave because her sister Hélène would be back any moment from her boyfriend's place, where she usually spent the night.

Later that morning, I went to the library, expecting to run into her – she was usually there around this time. But she was not there. It felt like she had disappeared from my life again. The weather was cold and grey. I sat there among the books, feeling empty. I wanted to touch her again, run my fingers through her hair, watch her smile, trace the contours of her body with my hands, look into her eyes and feel her love. I was staring down at a book, wallowing in self-pity, when suddenly I looked up and there she was, sitting across the table. Ah, I felt such relief, such joy.

'I was too tired to go to class this morning,' she explained. We sat there for some time, not saying much.

'Can I see you tonight?' I asked finally.

'All right, but not too late and not too long,' she said with her trademark shy smile.

That evening at her apartment, we kissed again that beautiful kiss. Slow and passionate. I took her to bed and we kissed some more. I took off my t-shirt, and then hers. She lay there on her back looking at me like she was in a trance. I kissed her breasts, under her breasts, on her stomach, and proceeded to undo her trousers. She didn't resist when I pulled them off. And the sight of those toned basketball thighs was to die for. I took off my turban and let my hair down à la Robert Plant. I kissed the insides of her thighs and went up to the tunnel of love. She moaned and dug her fingers in my hair. That night, we went all the way.

I left around six in the morning. She left for her parents' house that day. She was gone for fifteen days. Those were the loneliest two weeks of my life.

They say solitude stimulates the mind. Not just the mind. Back in India, at the DAV college library, I had read a few pages of a Milan Kundera novel in which the young protagonist, living a sad life, is averse to the idea of sexual gratification by self-stimulation. I used to think along the same lines, but that evening curiosity got the better of me. I was sitting on the edge of my little bed in the tiny room at the students' hostel. It was hot. I was alone and bored, Gisèle was away, so I decided to indulge in some self-exploration. I had no urge to play, but I thought, Let's give it a try, apparently it's good practice for sex. It makes you blind, but not the first time. So why not practise and become perfect and be ready to please Gisèle when she returned. I uncovered my cock and looked at it with no desire. I didn't even know where to begin. I was naïve then and unaware of the technique of self-pleasure. I stroked myself into a hard-on and put on a condom to avoid sticky fingers. It turned out to be a long and tiring task for my right hand, and a frustrating one for my right brain. I didn't come and abandoned the exercise. But practice would make perfect.

4

One evening in June, the phone rang in the corridor on the second floor of Cuffon Pavot. I answered it with some anticipation and a female voice said she wanted to speak to me. It was Gisèle! My two-week prayer had been answered. She was back and wanted to see me. I went crazy with joy. On my way to her apartment, I stopped by a house with beautiful red roses in the front yard, pushed the buzzer and asked the owner if I could pick a rose. The old lady said, 'Yes, if it pleases you.'

It certainly pleased Gisèle. We spent all evening talking, caressing, making love, drinking tea and munching on cookies. We danced to my cassette tape of rock 'n' roll hits. It was a little dream come true. I had always wanted to rock 'n' roll with a beautiful girl on a wooden floor. She laughed a lot that day. It was a perfect summer evening.

The later evenings were not so perfect. You see, Gisèle did not want to leave her boyfriend, so officially, she and I were just friends. We couldn't go out freely and make out like lovers. Angers is a small town and her sister or someone would see us and either label her a slut or tell her boyfriend. And if she made out with the only guy with a turban in Angers, she'd be caught quicker than it took me to tie the turban. We couldn't always hook up at her apartment because her sister was there. So the next time we wanted to be together, she came to my room at the hostel. I wanted to make love but she was not into it.

'I feel guilty,' she said.

'I love you,' I replied.

'I like you very much,' she said, 'but we should stop this.'

'No, please don't say that. I love you. Do you not care for me?'

'I do,' she said and tears welled up in her eyes.

That killed my appetite. We lay in my tiny bed, my head on her bosom. Then I accompanied her home and we spent another hour in the corridor kissing and whispering in each other's ears.

'I love you.'

'I like you.'

'Will I see you again?'

'Yes, but only as friends.'

That made me sad.

June 21 marks the official start of summer in France and the French celebrate *fête de la musique*, a country-wide music festival. It's a day when local bands in every city go out and perform in the streets. Professional bands, amateur bands, teen bands, kids' bands and a lot of shitty bands play all over town. Bars and cafés organize gigs and the entire city is out on the street. The main pedestrian streets get clogged with sweaty human bodies. That year on June 21, I was out in the streets checking out the bands. I had asked Gisèle to come with me but she said she had to study for her exams and I hadn't insisted, I wanted to give her space. I think she was trying to put some distance between us. So there I was in the crowded streets, feeling lovelorn, passing by kissing lovers, envying them. A local blues band was playing at Place du Pilori. The harp player was really good. The street was jam-packed. I stood in the middle of the crowd, feeling blue.

I had been standing there ten minutes when I felt a nudge on my back. I turned around, there was nobody I knew, just people struggling to pass this way or that. Then I noticed a hand in the air and a face behind other faces, beckoning me. It was so crowded she couldn't get any closer. It was amazing how she even noticed me in that crowd. It was Gisèle. I can't describe the way I felt on seeing her. A man with a secret love will know.

'How did you find me in this crowd?' I asked as I finally made my way to her.

'I was looking for a black turban around the blues,' she smiled. She was on her way back home after an errand.

'I'll walk you home.'

On our way, we were stopped outside a bar by a jolly, bear-like guy with a drink in his hand. He said in English, 'Man, are you Sikh? I love Sikhs, my best friend is Sikh.' He was a young engineer from Sweden working at Scania. I said, Nice to meet you, hope to run into you again, and took my leave. I always ran into people who knew me or wanted to get to know me because they thought I was Indian or Pakistani or Iranian or Sikh or some such exotic species. At her door, not meaning to impose, I began to take my leave.

'Come up for a drink.'

I wasn't going to refuse. She made lemonade. We made small talk. My lemonade finished, I asked if she wanted me to leave. She said I could stay and read magazines while she studied. I sat at the metal table with a women's magazine and watched her sitting in bed trying to study while a band played just outside. They were playing good music. I said I wanted to go down and listen to it for a few minutes. She didn't mind. The crowd was thinner here. I spotted a couple of Indian guys from my class and felt an urge to brag that I was spending the evening with my beautiful girlfriend. I wanted to point to the window and say, There, that's where my love awaits me. I just nodded at them.

I was back in the apartment in less than fifteen minutes. Gisèle told me to come and sit in bed with her. So I sat with her and began to read an article about eroticism in art. I was laboriously wading through the second paragraph of the article when she put down her book and turned to me. Her hand slid between my legs.

'Hey, you're supposed to study for your exam,' I said.

'I know, but I'm too distracted right now.'

'You're going to blame me for distracting you.'

'Don't worry, I'll blame the loud music outside,' she said playfully, caressing my manhood.

I slipped my hand through her hair and brought her mouth to mine, and we kissed that long passionate kiss that was the highlight of this relationship.

'Give me your tongue,' I whispered. She did.

I sucked her tongue and my hand purposefully wandered over her back and under her pants. She sighed. I kissed her neck, taking in the fragrance of her hair. I unbuttoned her shirt, fondled her breasts and nibbled on her nipples as she continued to stroke me. I kissed her stomach, and licked and sucked her navel. She giggled. I kissed along her waist, undid her pants and pulled them off. Then I flipped her over, climbed on her back and dug my hands into her hair. I smelled her hair, sucked her neck, nibbled at her earlobes and caressed and kissed her back down to the end of her spine. She moaned in approval. My mouth lingered on the arch of her back. Then in one smooth move, I slid off the yellow panties, saying, '*Baisse ta culotte, c'est moi qui pilote.*' Panties down I demand, I'm the one in command. She burst into laughter. 'I believe I am not the only one helping you with your French, Monsieur Singh,' she said teasingly. I bent down and kissed every pixel of her beautiful ass. Then I lay on her back, breathing in the summer scent of her body and gently riding her derrière.

When I climbed off her several minutes later, she had a naughty twinkle in her eye.

'It was good?' she enquired in English.

Oh yeah, it was good! So fucking good. My first *fête de la musique*, which had looked dry and gloomy at the outset, had ended up being so wet and juicy. *Fête de l'amour.* Thank you, Lord, for all the good things you bestow on this poor sinner in moments of despair.

Gisèle loved to go down on me. On one of my visits to her apartment, after making out some, she proceeded to do just that. She was wearing a pale blue cotton shirt that made her look like a soft candy I just had to touch, feel and squeeze. I stood there in my green corduroy trousers. The lights were low. She knelt down, undid my belt, unzipped the fly, slid her hand into my VIP underwear, and began to kiss and lick. A couple of minutes into the act, I observed that she was not concentrating. I wondered if she didn't like how it tasted today. Then she looked up at me, worried, and said,

'Hélène will be back any moment.' I said nothing, feeling bad at the prospect of having my pleasure nipped in the bud. She resumed kissing and sucking, probably feeling sorry for my situation.

I was enjoying the experience, looking at her giving her love to my VIP. A minute or two passed, then we heard the door. Gisèle jumped up, sprang to the study table, popped a chewing gum in her mouth and was out of the room in five seconds. I was left in the lurch and there was no time to hide, disappear or die. I pulled up my pants – thank god I hadn't taken them off completely – fastened my belt at the speed of lightning and met Hélène and her boyfriend François in the kitchen.

'*Salut, ça va?*' Kiss kiss. Gisèle got talking with them, and I realized that my fly was open. I half-turned and zipped it up. Hélène and François stayed only a few minutes, they had to go somewhere else. After they left, Gisèle gave me a sly smile of relief, led me back to bed and went back to loving the lucky little devil. I can still see her lips around my cock, her shy eyes, her dark brown hair against her soft blue shirt. My generative fluid came spurting out like lava from a volcano. It was amazing. She pulled her mouth away, grinning and wiping.

The next time I saw her, she told me that François had noticed my open fly and been suspicious. He also happened to be Gisèle's boyfriend's best friend. But Hélène had assured him that there was nothing between Gisèle and me, we were just friends. And that maybe my zipper was broken and Gisèle herself had a pair of pants with a broken zipper. Hélène had no due.

Soon the day came when I had to leave for my internship. I was sad that I was not going to see Gisèle for two months. We were both returning to Angers in September for the new school year. It never occurred to me what two months of separation could do to our secret relationship. I was still callow in the ways of the world.

My last night in Angers, I packed up half the stuff in my room and went to see Gisèle at about 10 p.m. We talked and had tea and cookies. I told her I still had a lot of packing to do, she said she would come down to the hostel to help. We were in the middle of this conversation when François showed up.

'I can't find Hélène.' He looked worried.

Gisèle jumped up. 'Don't worry, I'll come with you to look for her,' she said.

I said, 'Okay, *au revoir*.' What else could I say? I was just a friend in the eyes of the world and we had to keep our liaison secret, especially from Gisèle's boyfriend's best friend. It was so awkward and incomplete, that goodbye moment. Imagine saying adieu to your love without a kiss, let alone a night of love.

We got out of the apartment and François started down the winding stairs. As I turned to follow him, I felt a nudge on my elbow and Gisèle gingerly handed me a tiny piece of paper which, after a second of perplexity, I put into my pocket. She locked the door and down the stairs we went.

On my way back to the hostel, my heart aching, I looked at the piece of paper. It was a leaf torn off a notebook, in which she had scribbled 'Come back after packing'. Ah, a glimmer of hope in that moment of utter despair. I applauded her wicked presence of mind, rushed back to my room and tried to finish the rest of the packing as fast as I could. It was past one when I finally called her.

'All good?'

'*Oui*, all good,' she said. The coast was clear.

I went back to her. She told me that Hélène had gone to François's apartment that evening but he was not home and she didn't have the keys. So she sat down on the stairs and, for some reason, started sobbing. A passer-by tried to comfort her and invited her for a drink. Hélène was feeling so lonely that she accepted the offer, and they went to a nearby bar. He asked for her phone number and said that if he called her it would only be for sex. Hélène gave him Gisèle's mobile number. Then they parted ways and Hélène was back at François's door by the time Gisèle and François got there. Hélène told Gisèle the story in private. She felt guilty about having had a drink with a stranger. Gisèle told her not to worry, because every girl had a secret, and she herself had a secret... with me.

'What? You told her!' I almost fell out of bed.

'Don't worry,' she said laughing. 'It is a secret between sisters.'

I nodded.

That was our last night of love. It broke my heart to say goodbye to her.

I carried around that piece of paper for years and looked at it from time to time. It was a souvenir of love. Then one day I tore it into shreds.

5

A five-hour journey including one train change found me in Quimper, Brittany. I was going to be a trainee on a three-star campsite near the city. The proprietor's wife came to pick me up, a plain, mean-looking, heavily pregnant woman. It was early evening when we reached the campsite and the place was surrounded in gloom. Although the surroundings were nice – it was far away from the city and there was greenery all around – the atmosphere weighed on me. I felt alone and sad and really fucking bad. And that feeling never left me for the entire duration of my stay. Even though I met some nice people, karaoked in the bar and swam in the pool, it seemed like an eternity of suffering. There began my first truly unpleasant experience in France.

The owners of the campsite were a bourgeois family and the mansion they lived in was a classified monument. The couple were stuck-up Catholics for whom reproduction was a religious duty. They already had six young kids, all boys, and another one on the way. In the first week, I heard one of the regulars say to the woman half-jokingly, 'You can stop now.'

I had imagined I was going to be an *animateur* at the campsite, organizing fun activities for the tourists. But they posted me at reception and expected me to learn to use the reservation software that was so fucking not interesting. There were two Spanish girls who were also training at reception. The trainees were unpaid, which had made the proprietors recruit too many of us. There wasn't enough work to keep us all occupied. So I decided to sit in a corner and read a book. I wanted to use every spare minute to learn something new. My attitude miffed the proprietors.

Everybody hated them, by the way. I met two cool guys, Pat and Greg, one from Australia, the other from England. They were working for Eurocamp, which had installed mobile homes on the campsite. They got laid quite often, both with colleagues and with the tourists. Pat and Greg liked me – and not everybody did. Because of my dislike for the place, I was gloomy and morose most of the time, especially with my French colleagues. I was still reeling from my separation from Gisèle. I was desperately in love with her. I was so miserable that I rang her at her parents' house once and almost started crying on the phone. I even rang Gilles and wept. Yes, I literally wept, sentimental fool that I was. Gisèle wrote to me every alternate day and I waited for her letter every Wednesday and Friday. When there was no letter I felt blue. One Wednesday, I remember, it was a bank holiday so there was no letter and I expressed my frustration and disappointment in front of the other trainees in the kitchen by shouting, 'I hate this fucking country!'

Of course I only meant that I hated that there were too many bank holidays in this country. Gisèle's letters kept me going. In one of her letters she wrote that she showed my picture to her favourite cousin, who said I was good-looking. In another letter, she wrote that I said such poetic things that a Frenchman would never be able to say. I was a romantic back then. A result of over-exposure to Dev Anand songs. I sat in the bar every evening and poured out my soul into long letters. One of the tourists once asked me if I was doing some kind of school assignment!

In my brighter moments, I entertained guests in the bar, karaoking to 'Great Balls of Fire'. I was pretty good too. An unshaven Jerry Lee Lewis in black turban. One evening, as I was engrossed in writing a letter to my sweetheart, a teenage Dutch girl came over to me, and asked if I was going to do 'Great Balls of Fire'. I said I hadn't planned on it.

'Please, I've specially asked my mom to come over and hear you do it. It's her favourite song,' she pleaded. 'It's her birthday.'

I really wasn't feeling up to it but I didn't want to disappoint her either, so I did the karaoke. It was one of my lesser performances, but it made the girl and her mother happy.

The only person I made friends with at the campsite was Marine: tall, short blond hair, nice ass, cute face, full of charm and with a great sense of humour. The only laughs I had in that godforsaken place were shared with her. She was at reception as well and I liked to be there when she was. She liked me and I would have loved to get intimate with her, but it was not meant to be. Besides the fact that she was much taller, she had a jealous boyfriend. I don't know how a free-spirited person like her ended up with a stuck-up asshole like that. Maybe opposites do attract. It was thanks to him that Marine and I couldn't keep in touch after I left. I told her about Gisèle. Not the whole truth, though. I told her I had a girlfriend called Gisèle, and it was a complicated relationship, and that I felt it was coming to an end. I was embarrassed to tell her that my girlfriend was in fact somebody else's girlfriend, and that I was just the backdoor man. Marine in turn told my story to Christine.

Now Christine had been working at the campsite for two or three summers. She was slim, one or two inches taller than me, wore glasses, looked like a nerd and had a fantastic ass. It was full, round and tight, a perfect pear. Christine worked at the reception too and slept on-site, just like myself and the Spanish trainees. I saw her every day – in fact, she was the first person I spoke to on my first day on the campsite. We shared a common dislike of the place.

In my second week there, the employees and trainees went for an after-work drink in Greg and Pat's tent. We had a good time, drinking wine and eating peanuts. Somebody left, somebody else said, 'See you later alligator,' which prompted me to put on my rock 'n' roll tape. I always carried it on me. The song that came out of the little stereo was Bill Haley's 'See You Later Alligator'. Everyone laughed. There was this stray cat in the tent cuddling up to Greg. I was not at all into cats then. I thought of cats as filthy stray animals that you shooed on sight. So I shooed it away and was chided by Christine.

'Dude, you should apologize,' said Pat in mock righteousness. 'Get down on your knees and apologize.'

I got down on my knees and asked for Christine's forgiveness.

'Okay, I'm not going to have you beheaded,' said Christine. We did a high-five. I sat on the couch next to her for the rest of the evening, sipping red wine...

I woke up in the morning to find myself lying on the couch under a blanket. Greg and Pat were snoring. Everyone else had left. The last thing I remembered of the evening was that I had laid my wine-weary head on Christine's shoulder and she was cool with it. That, I think, was a very good start.

A few evenings later, all of us campsite workers went to a nearby discotheque. Pat, Christine and I sat by the pool there, talking about who liked whom in our little community of campsite employees and trainees. They were talking, I was listening. Graziella fancied Greg, Lizzie fancied Greg too, Nicolas liked Camilla...

'And you, who do you like?' Christine said to me in English. I stared at her like a dumbass. I hadn't thought about it.

'He likes you!' said Pat, patting her knee.

'But I like cats,' she said, making a cute face and looking down at the floor. Pat and I laughed. It was a clear sign that she had a soft spot for me. And very likely if I was nice to cats she would play house with my mouse. But blinded by my heartache for Gisèle, I failed to react. Besides, she was always aloof and cold. She never made a direct move. Probably because Marine had told her about Gisèle. And in the last few weeks of my time there, our relationship, if you can call it that, went downhill. I can see now that it was my uncaring, indifferent attitude that bugged Christine. I was not a team player and I was not like the others. But really, that was because I was all tangled up in my own blues, constantly suffering inside.

More about Christine in a minute. First, here's an account of a big cock-tease that I underwent at the campsite. There were these two English girls vacationing with their parents, looking for some love. A couple of times they came over to me for chit-chat. Everybody wanted to get to know me in those days. They were good-looking and sassy, total trouser arousers. One was slim and the other one had rounded features. I preferred the rounded one, but I'd take either. The slim one had eyes for me. One late evening, after celebrating their nineteenth birthday together, they made a bet with the other teenagers on the campsite that they would get into the cold swimming pool. And they did get into the pool, with just their underwear on. Their friends applauded, then went back to the bar. I hovered near the pool. Like a bee around a honeycomb, like a dog around a bone. These two cold-water mermaids put on their clothes and came over to speak to me. They were very excited about their feat, shivering with excitement and cold.

'You must be totally wet under your clothes,' I said.

'No, not really, I'm wearing a thong, it's doesn't get wet... here, feel my ass and see for yourself,' the slim one said, projecting her protuberance my way. I hesitated for a second then cupped one hemisphere of her ass with my hand.

'Here, touch mine too,' the round one said and I felt her ass too. If this happened to me today, I'd say to them, 'You ladies deserve a warm massage. Let's go to your tent.' But that evening, I didn't know what to say. They wished me goodnight and went back to their tent. I went back to my room and pitched a tent of my own. Thrice. That's my record – three solo shots in a span of two hours. I kept imagining their asses and shooting my load into a rag, torn off an old turban.

I burnt in the fires of envy when I learnt that the day before they left, the nubile nymphs had their cherries popped by the two young studs in the kitchen. The round one had a pierced vagina, the insider informed me.

Just before I left, I had a full-fledged fight with Christine. She deliberately started it. To cut a long story short, Christine had organized a farewell soirée for the Spanish trainees. Everybody was invited and was expected to bring wine to the party. I didn't really want to party so I arrived only towards the end of the evening and didn't bring wine. I had expected the party to be over by the time I arrived. The next day, my rosé disappeared from the fridge. At lunch, I went to the bar to get a glass of wine and found my bottle of rosé sitting at the bar, half empty, in between Christine and Danielle, the barmaid. I didn't know how to react. I asked, 'Can I have some of that wine?'

'*Non*,' shot back Christine.

I said it was my wine, she said it wasn't, I said it was and the voices went up. Danielle pushed both of us into the room at the back of the bar and we continued to shout at each other. Christine admitted it was my wine and that she had taken it to teach me a lesson. At one point she pushed me because I got too loud. Finally I stormed out, yelling, 'Fucking bitch! That fucking bitch!' A tourist sitting with a glass of beer at the bar looked up at me in surprise.

Once I had calmed down, I felt bad. I am basically a decent guy, you know. The next day, I confronted Christine again at the bar, nicely this time. I said I was sorry but I wanted to know why she had deliberately provoked me. She didn't say anything.

I said in French, 'What's the reason, tell me why are you so mean to me? You in love with me?'

'*Non*,' she said, shaking her head resignedly. I let her be. A few days later, she left.

And so did I. It was mid-August. Marine and her boyfriend drove me to the station, and I was off to Angers, high and dry. Everybody in France gets laid on a campsite at least once in their life. Only schmucks like me don't. Actually, even schmucks get laid on a campsite, I'm beneath a schmuck. Pat's farewell words were, 'Hey, ready to leave? Must be eager to jump into bed with your girlfriend. You haven't had it in a while.'

Friends, losers and countrymen, the lesson here is this: don't fall in love. Love makes you blind and useless. It numbs your senses and kills your skirt-chasing instincts. Instead, be open and ready to take on any sexual possibilities, 'coz sex is all around you. And an opportunity to get laid is a gift you must not refuse. So don't be a schmuck, and always keep your eyes, ears, mind and fly open to accommodate a potential prospect.

Gilles met me at the station. He took me to his apartment and said I could stay with him until I found a place of my own. I slept on the comfortable leather couch in the living room, next to a wooden chest that Gilles had restored. It was his hobby, he restored wooden chests and antique watches. I had a good time at Gilles's, though his girlfriend was not too pleased that I was staying there. I tried to go out during the day to look for a room to rent. I also enrolled at the University of Angers for a second year of *licence* in English.

I would return in the evening and Gilles would cook dinner. I insisted on doing the dishes. We talked about life, love and Gisèle.

After a month, Gilles said I had to go – his love life was on the rocks. It was the last week of September. I called Francis, my friend from ESTHUA, and asked if I could stay with him for a few days. He agreed. Francis shared a big apartment with two other guys. Relieved, I continued my search for a cheap room to rent, poring over the newspaper, looking for *A LOUER* signs, checking with the student service, even asking people on the street. I was starting to feel the weight of life.

Now that ESTHUA was over, I was alone and the daunting task of fending for myself lay ahead. Not that the ESTHUA folks had been particularly helpful but theoretically I had been their responsibility. Now the responsibility was solely mine. Enrolment at uni would get my visa renewed for a year but I had to find a place to live and a job to pay the rent. I also needed to figure out where I was headed, what I was going to do with my life, and how I would help my mother financially. If I ever made it, that is. I was worried and felt helpless. And I missed Gisèle terribly. I had her cell number but I didn't want to call because in her last letter she wrote that she would call me when she got back to Angers. I did wonder why she still had not got in touch with me. The school year had started and she must have been in town since mid-September. I missed her very much.

A week later, I spotted her at the university campus at St Serge. I didn't go up to her. I was not sure what I would say to her, whether I'd kiss her on the cheek or on the mouth, play it cool or take her in my arms and say 'I love you' a hundred times. A day passed, and I called her cell phone. She gave me her address.

What a relief it was to be with her again, alone. We exchanged a formal four-peck kiss.

'I am thirsty,' I said and proceeded to drink from her lips. She stopped me firmly. Things had changed. She had decided to be faithful to her boyfriend, they had reconciled their differences that summer. As you can imagine, I felt bad, really really bad. I had spent three months weeping and pining for a touch of those lips, and now that they were three inches in front of me, I was not allowed to get any closer!

'That's not fair, you're being cruel,' I said. She pressed her lips together and shrugged as only the French do. I felt heartbroken. I had been going to the American library and reading *The Art of Tantric Sex* to learn to please her in extraordinary ways. The light in her apartment was dim and yellow, adding to the gloom in my heart. If I remember right, we talked a bit about us, about me, about them, and I felt miserable the whole time. Then I left, feeling alone and unloved. I suspect her feelings for me would not have changed so radically if I had been a better lover.

Francis and his friends were regular church-goers and invited me to attend Mass with them the following Sunday. It was an unforgettable experience. It was a Baptist church, housed in a nondescript building opposite a car park. The pastor gave his sermon, made some happy announcements about this and the other, and asked the Lord Jesus Christ to bless us all. A plate was passed around with some sort of dried bread, which represented the body of Christ. Then everybody stood up and sang songs. And there, in the middle of singing, I started weeping uncontrollably. My pain at being so alone, my sense of deep failure flowed out through those tears. I tried not to be noisy and I don't think anybody noticed. After Mass, the attendees set up tables and brought in food and we all sat down to eat with lots of jokes and laughter. It was potluck and everybody had brought something to the table. Salads, pies, tarts and delicious cakes. It made me feel a lot better. That afternoon, I told Francis and his flatmate Stéphane what had happened and they said it often did when you went to church for the first time.

The following week, I was feeling very low and went to see Gisèle. We talked, it was late, I asked if I could stay and she said yes for auld lang syne. I spent the night in her bed, trying to coax her into making love while she tried to sleep. Finally she gave me a half-asleep pity hand job. I didn't sleep at all that night. A few days later, I went to see her again, unannounced, all depressed and close to tears. She was expecting her boyfriend and didn't let me in. That was the last time I saw her. I think I realized at that point how pathetic I was and that was the end of the story. Nonetheless, for a long time I pined to kiss her one last time. Only a slow kiss would give this relationship proper closure.

6

Mid-October. I finally found a room I could afford to rent. I called the landlord and he agreed to let me the room and asked me to come and see him. I telephoned the next day to say I was coming, but the lady said she had rented the room to someone else.

'What! How could you do this to me? I'm going to have to live on the sidewalk now. Your husband said it was okay, and you're telling me you rented the room to someone else?'

She said she was sorry. I hung up, crestfallen. Then I thought, no way, I was not going to let them do this to me, and left for their house. It was a fifteen-minute walk from the city centre. The lady answered the door. I had only started to say who I was when she said, 'Yes, yes, come in, I'm sorry, but it's okay. I had a chat with my husband. We'll let you the room. The other girl is not coming immediately, anyway.'

What a relief that was. You literally have to go the distance for whatever you want in life. And not take no for an answer, at least not the first time. In the next two days, with a little help from my friends, I moved into my room on rue St Léonard. The house was a typical, three-storied *maison angevine*, owned by a retired couple, and I had a lovely wood-floored room on the top floor. It had a writing table, a single bed, a narrow wooden chest next to the bed with a whiskey bottle converted into a lamp and a large armoire. There was a little annexe with a dresser, which I used as my kitchen-cum-wardrobe. It was quite a bit of room for little old me. I put up postcards, magazine cutouts and photographs of Charlie Parker, Dev Anand and Camus, and handwritten messages like '*J'aime meiux tes lèvres que mes livres*', by Jacque Prévert.

The landlords were kind to me. They were an old bourgeois couple and apparently the only family in the area to bear their name with that spelling. They had three good-looking sons, all married with wives and children, good jobs and houses of their own. Most of the week Monsieur and Madame were away in their country house or on vacation abroad and I would be left alone in the big house. I don't know how they could leave their house with somebody they barely knew. I certainly wouldn't.

University started and I got busy. The classes were crap – they taught English in French, a total waste of time. But it did give me another year's visa. Besides, I met a lot of interesting people. And I got laid.

It was an afternoon in late October. I climbed aboard a crowded bus bound for the city centre and found myself standing opposite this girl with short, dirty-blond hair. She smiled at me nervously and made some remarks about it being stuffy and crowded. I agreed. It was a hot October. Then she got off the bus. By the time the bus reached Ralliement, it was almost empty. I found myself a seat near the back and was just sitting down when I found myself facing the dirty blonde. It was surreal. Where did she get on the bus again! She smiled and sat down next to me.

'Where do you live?' I asked.

'On Rue St Jacques.' I didn't know where that was and didn't care.

The bus was not moving yet.

'I should go,' she said and gave me a big kiss on the cheek before she got off the bus.

In France, men and women who know each other kiss on the cheek, it's a light peck, one or two on each cheek. Lovers kiss on the mouth. And this girl, whom I'd just stood opposite in the bus and barely spoken to, had no reason at all to kiss me, much less a non-standard, single kiss with her mouth fully pressed against my cheek. I was flattered, and perplexed.

A few days later I bumped into her again at the Belle-Beille campus. We said bonjour and she gave me the same over-affectionate kiss on one cheek. The following week I saw her again and she said I should have dinner with her. The next day, we met at the library and took the bus to her studio. She made chicken scallops with fresh cream and green peas. As we ate, she told me about her boyfriend and how much she loved and missed him. He had had a terrible motorcycle accident and was in the hospital. She said he occupied her heart and her soul. I felt weird and braced myself for a serious cock-whack. Maybe she only wanted someone to talk to.

As I was saying goodbye, she gave me the same full-mouthed kiss on one cheek.

'Why do you kiss me like that?'

'Oh, you don't want me to?'

I answered by sliding my hands around her waist and pressing my mouth to hers. Then I sat on a stool, made her sit astride me, we kissed some more and I took off her shirt. Her breasts were long and pointy, the kind I am not crazy about. But I praised them and said sweet nothings to her, just to make sure I got into her pants. She didn't want to fuck the first night. I came back the next night and we fucked, although it did take some more persuasion. She was starting to feel guilty about cheating on her ailing boyfriend and was having a 'to fuck or not to fuck' crisis. She dilly-dallied but I managed to convince her that a fuck would do her good and give her the strength to stand by her man. She seemed to understand. The next minute, I hopped into bed, lay spread-eagled and politely asked her to suck my dick. She said she wasn't very good at it. I told her not to worry and to do what she could. She sucked for a couple of minutes. It was good. I told her to stop when I was close. Then I pinned her back to the bed, put on a condom and went right in. Her legs automatically went up in the air and she started moaning. '*Ah, ah, ah... oui, oui, oui, comme ça, comme ça... plus vite, plus vite...*' I didn't dig noisy women then. Yes, yes, I was stupid. I came sooner than expected, the first shot is always too quick. I should have let her finish the blow job.

Let me tell you that there was nothing extraordinary about this girl, except her devotion to her boyfriend. She wanted to fuck because she needed to, you know, it's a basic human need, after all. And she wanted to fuck me because she thought I was good-looking and charming. It was a clear case of lust at first sight. I didn't go back to her a second time. She was rather plain to look at and talked too much. I was arrogant in those days, and thought all I needed was a little fucking to get back my confidence and wash away the frustration of the past months. I would find someone else soon.

Wishful thinking. I did not respect what the Lord had put on my plate and I was confident he would give me more. The Lord, on the other hand, was trying to tell me that if I wanted more and better, I had to first cherish what I had and show some gratitude. It took me a while to learn that. For all ye losers out there, there is power in appreciation and thankfulness. I learnt that from the many self-improvement books I used to read. When you appreciate what you have, you get more of it.

By November it had become cold and rainy. I found an apple-picking job in Lion d'Angers. I needed a raincoat for the job, but didn't want to buy one. Then I ran into Julie, whom I had met a few days before at Bar du Centre, and she said she could lend me her raincoat. I went to work at six in the morning, with a guy who was driving there. Got fired on the first day because they said I was too slow. I hated the work, anyway. I got back home feeling light and chirpy. I didn't have to wake up the next morning to go to a muddy apple orchard in the drizzle. I was whistling to myself when there was a knock on the door. An elegant young girl in a plaid skirt stood at my doorstep. Her hair was short and reddish-brown, just like Gisèle's.

'Bonjour,' I said. 'You must be the new neighbour the landlord told me about, in the room downstairs.'

'Yes, I am Colline, I arrived last week.'

I invited her in. Colline was from Nantes and didn't know Angers very well. I asked her to come and have a drink with me.

On our way to Bar du Centre we talked, or rather I talked. I told her about Gisèle and my heartbreak, perhaps in an attempt to garner sympathy. This was one of my big flaws. I talked too much, revealed too much too soon, no mystery left, nothing more than met the eye, no intrigue, no bait... What an idiot.

At the bar, we had a pleasant, balanced conversation. She was preparing for CAPES at the uni in Nantes and had some classes at the Catholic University in Angers on Tuesday and Wednesday. When we were about to pay for our drinks, Ahmed, the bar owner, started saying something about India. He looked a bit drunk. I think he said something about Indian food and drink and about going to India.

'Yeah, if you come to India, you won't forget our hospitality,' I said.

'Speaking of hospitality, your drinks are on the house. That's Iranian hospitality for you,' said Ahmed.

'What, really?'

He nodded. I thanked him and we left.

'Well, that's never happened to me before!' said Colline in surprise. 'A drink on the house in a bar? No way. Just doesn't happen in France.'

'You should go out with me more,' I said.

I was on the second floor, she was on the first, right under me. In the morning, as I was coming down the stairs, I shouted, 'Hey Colline, it's a beautiful morning.' She said something from inside her room. I was off. That evening, I asked if she fancied going out again, but she was busy. So I called Julie, and we met up at Bar du Centre twenty minutes later. We had wine and a pleasant conversation about my life in India and my life in France, and then she offered to drop me home. I said I preferred to walk. I didn't want to take advantage of her kindness. What a moron.

The next week, Colline was free and we went out for a drink again. I was beginning to like her, but then I'm easy to please. We had a nice conversation, and among other things, I said that I might be falling in love with her. I said that partly because I thought it was true and partly to see her reaction. 'You'd change your mind if you saw me in my pyjamas,' she said with a laugh.

Of course, I wanted to see her without pyjamas. Unfortunately, nothing of that sort happened. After the drink we just walked back home and went into our respective rooms. The next day she was off to Nantes for two weeks. Before she left I tried to kiss her goodbye on the lips, but she turned her face away. I felt rejected and spent the rest of the day drifting from bar to bar, wallowing in self-pity. I had fucked up with Colline. When I came back home in the evening, I found a little plastic pot of yogurt on my doorstep, with a note from Colline: 'This is going to expire before my return.'

So she doesn't hate me, this might work still. Thank you, God, I said, smiling at the ceiling.

Two weeks went by, and my beautiful neighbour was back. She came up to see me, I tried to kiss her again, she left. And stopped speaking to me. I asked her why, she said something like 'you don't know your limits', or 'you don't know when to stop'. That made me feel bad. I knew my fantasy was over, and so it was. For the rest of the year we maintained a distant neighbourliness. I didn't go downstairs to see her, she didn't come up to see me. I just heard her door open and close and the sound of the toilet and the shower. We shared the same shower and it was on my floor. I liked to think it was *my* shower that I shared with her.

From time to time, she left me notes about too much noise from my room, if I played a CD too loud or paced up and down the wooden floor. Sometimes I wrote back. I have to make a confession: sometimes I was deliberately loud because I wanted her attention. I wanted her to feel my presence and know that I was in love with her. I feel bad about it now, I really do, it was such immature behaviour. I wish I remembered her last name so I could look her up on Facebook and apologize. And explain to her that the night she could not sleep because of the music from my room, it wasn't because the music was loud, it was because the CD player lay on the floor and the sound seeped through the wood. Forgive me, Colline.

You must have realized by now how blind, stupid and down on luck I was when it came to sex. So Colline was a disaster, but at the same time there was Julie. And Julie was always happy to hear from me. She was cute, her breasts were big and her ass exactly like Kate Winslet's in *Romance and Cigarettes*. Every time I called her for a drink, she came, just like Gisèle used to. And after drinks she offered to drive me home. She was my proverbial silver lining. But how can you see the silver lining when your stupid eyes are wide shut?

Julie and I must've gone out for drinks at least four times, and every single time I refused to be driven home by her. Can you believe that? I thought she was just being kind and I didn't want her to go through the trouble. I should have known better. Any idiot with a pair of eyes would see that she was kind to me because she liked me. She was expecting me to return the raincoat favour with a raincoat. All I needed to do was let her drive me home and ask her in for a cuppa. I will always remain perplexed about my idiocy with her. I don't know what was going on in my head, I didn't even think about it until it was too late.

Soon it became difficult to get hold of Julie, either at uni or on the phone. When I ran into her a few weeks later, she barely even looked at me. I suppose she had rejected me as a lost cause and moved on. Time and tail wait for none.

So once again, fellow losers, the lesson here is to be awake, aware and watchful. When the iron is hot, strike. When the pussy is wet, dive. Carpe fucking diem. Don't wait and don't think too much. In my experience, guys who think too much don't get that much. And beware of that shitty little thing called love. I know, I know, it's beautiful while it lasts, but it begins to stink the moment your lover moves on, leaving you behind.

2001

7

I met a lot of people this year. Some became friends and helped me in little ways. Others enjoyed talking with me and bought me drinks. They all wanted to know about my exotic country – the poverty, the castes, the untouchables, the holy cow, the monsoon, the heat, Gandhi and all that jazz.

I met Rémi Boncoeur. He was studying modern literature at the university, and we hung out a lot. We mooched around town like dingledodies, yakety-yaking about everything and eyeballing the beauties. '*Discret!*' Rémi would keep telling me, embarrassed by the way I openly ogled at girls.

We went to Bar du Centre every other day. Rémi had recently had a break-up and hadn't met anyone new yet. He always bought our drinks. Rémi knew a lot about cinema, literature and poetry. He would recite Baudelaire's erotic verses in his inimitable style – fluent, funny and creepy at the same time. In his voluble moments, he sounded like a French Dean Moriarty. We talked about jazz, the Beat Generation and the babes, Rémi wondered how a guy from India came to be so interested in jazz and Jack Kerouac. And the fact that I was gung-ho on the female ass mystified my friend further. To him the main appeal in a woman's body was her face. Right, what a hypocrite.

We were a pair of randy bastards. Our unspent energies found a creative outlet in the recycling of romantic classics:

'Someday my princess will come… and give me a blow job', 'Suck me tender suck me blue, never let me go… without a blow'.

I met a lot of girls that I wanted to jazz but nothing ever happened. I was good at approaching them but always failed to seal the deal. Audrey, Rachel, Elodie, Paula… and this girl I met through Rémi. Agnès. The three of us had drinks together, and a few days later I bumped into her on the bus from Belle-Beille to the city centre. She invited me over for coffee.

We got off at her stop and walked over to her tiny studio apartment. She prepared to brew coffee, teasing me about my accent as she pottered about. She wore dark-framed glasses and was slightly on the heavier side. When she leaned over I caught a glimpse of her breasts – they were like succulent oranges waiting to be pressed.

The coffee was still brewing when I remembered that I had to be at my new job in half an hour. Bummer. Agnès walked me back to the bus stop. She was into me, I could tell by her body language. And who has the time and will to spontaneously invite you over for coffee and then walk you back to the bus stand? Only a chick who wants your dick. But once again, I lacked the drive to grab the occasion. I didn't even ask for her phone number before leaving, too eager to be on time at the chicken-delivery job. I never ran into her again. For the next six months, I delivered fried chicken all over Angers on a mobilette with a helmet worn over my turban, in the freezing cold and under pouring rain.

Finally, in February, the Lord decided to reward me after all the lovelessness I had been through and put a tall, sultry brunette in my path. Did I mention how totally I dig tall chicks, with their generously endowed bodies and ample asses? All that surface area to play in. Besides, with my size, I don't have much choice. They are all taller than me. And as far as my experience goes, French women are pretty open-minded about the size and looks of their man.

I first spotted her at the library in the beginning of the year. Rather, she spotted me. I caught her staring at me through her à la mode eye-glasses. Girls in glasses make horny lasses. She was sitting a couple of desks away. From what I could see, she looked juicy and full-bodied. Those boobs looked delicious. She gave a nervous smile when I looked at her. I'm not sure if I smiled back. A lot of women happened to stare and smile at me, it didn't mean all of them wanted to get it on with the little unshaven turban-bearer. Or maybe they did, I don't know.

Another time, I saw her at the university restaurant just as I was telling Rémi about her. When she got up at the end of the meal, her chair fell to the floor, dragged down by the weight of her coat and handbag. Rémi and I laughed. She noticed. I didn't think I was going to get laid with her, it seemed too good to be true. She was tall and buxom, naturally tanned and had a narrow slit between her two front teeth – the hallmark of horny harlots – and had the sort of reserved demeanour that slutty girls put on to appear virtuous. The kind you absolutely have to get to know from the inside. And the ass she had... wow!

Many evenings later, while I was on my way to the city centre, I saw the sultry brunette walking down the street, just outside city hall. I seized the moment and said good evening.

'Bonsoir,' she replied. She looked pleasantly surprised. I said we had seen each other at university. She pretended to try to remember for a second, and then nodded. We walked down the street together. She asked me where I came from and how come I spoke French so well. She praised my French in a voice that made me think she was a potential lay. But somehow, when we reached the point where our ways parted, I just shook her hand like a gentleman with no balls and said, 'Au revoir.' Her name was Florence.

I saw her again at uni after February holidays. We said hello, how was the holiday, and as we said au revoir she asked me for my number. That's the only time a girl ever asked me for my number. We met up that very evening. She wore a long black coat and knee-high black boots with heels and looked hot. I loved the way she stooped to kiss me on the cheek. We had a drink at a café and then, at her suggestion, strolled up to the Jardin du Mai, just across from city hall. In the garden, she wanted to sit down on a bench. It was cold and the benches were wet with dew. Seeing my hesitation, she fished out a Kleenex and wiped the dew off the bench. It was still wet but I sat down. We talked and I wondered if I should kiss her. Then I had a better idea, I said I lived close by and we could go to my place for something warm to drink. She agreed. Back in my room, I made myself a cup of tea, she just had water.

'I like your room,' she said, glancing around at the pictures and postcards on the walls. 'There is disorder here, but at the same time there is an order.' It was the most ridiculous pseudo-intellectual crap I had ever heard. Still makes me laugh. She sat on the chair and I sat on the edge of my bed. We talked until four in the morning, with the Joe Henderson trio playing softly in the background. Then she said she'd better go otherwise her mother would freak out. I accompanied her downstairs, and we tried not to make the wooden staircase creak – Colline was probably asleep in her room. We proceeded to say goodbye in the usual French fashion, one kiss on the left cheek... one kiss on the right... one on the left... one on the right... then my hands were on her shoulders and my mouth was on hers. We kissed for a minute, and I started to unbutton her coat.

'I'm going to be cold,' she said.

'I'll warm you up.'

We kissed again and I let her sit on the wooden chest by the door. Then my hands explored her body. When they reached inside her pants, she said the situation was getting hot and she had to leave before it got out of hand. French chicks are often fussy about fucking on the first night. They don't want to be thought of as a *fille facile*, an easy lay, a round heel, you know. The second time she came to my place she was wearing a short beige skirt that flattered her sumptuous ass, accentuated by black tights. I had spotted her in the street once with that skirt on. She was with a burly black guy and it looked like they were going to fuck. Maybe she wore that skirt when she was going to fuck. It was her fuck-skirt. She came in, we kissed, then I turned on the music while she looked around and stood by my desk looking at the English language books.

'You're fortunate to be bilingual,' she said. I was just fortunate to be standing behind her, looking at her splendid behind.

I reached out and put my hands on her hips. Her body tensed, I squeezed a little and let my hands slide down her thighs, reach the hem of the skirt and travel upwards, underneath the skirt, feeling the flesh through the fabric of her tights. We got out of our clothes in stages. She wore fine lingerie. She lay on the bed, I kissed her breasts, then turned her over and sat astride her back. I covered her back with wet kisses all the way from the neck down to the end of her spine. 'Mmm... where did you learn that?' she whispered. I touched her wetness and entered from the rear. Pure animal lust. Contrary to expectation, she didn't make much noise. My bed did. The fucking was good, though I suspected I came just a teeny bit too soon. But she looked happy.

In our post-coital conversation, she said I was handsome and that a friend of hers agreed. She and her friend both thought I was handsome, can you believe that? We hooked up a few more times after that. And then it came to an end. It didn't have to end so soon. It was once again my arrogance playing havoc with good sense. You see, while she had a gorgeous body and the most tempting smile, she fancied herself as an intellectual and spoke way too much – before and after sex. I found that really irritating. Also, she smelled weird down there. That turned me off to the point where I couldn't get it up any more. I tried to keep her happy with my fingers. Dad called just then and I spoke to him with two fingers of my right hand still inside her. It was as if I was facilitating a long-distance spiritual connection between dad and Flo's fanny. Gross! Gross! Gross! Then I made myself a cup of tea and sat in bed sipping. She lay on my left, in all her natural tan glory. So I'm sipping tea in my favourite cup, she's lying very close, recuperating. Then her head moves, she starts kissing me, on the chest, nipples, going lower with each kiss, on the stomach, along the waistband of my boxers. Then she lowered the elastic and kissed the base of the cock. I was hard and ready to rock. She kissed and nibbled the length, the tip, then swallowed the whole thing. She held it steady with one hand and lollipopped it, looking at me with half closed eyes, her hair brushing my thighs. It was a beautiful sight. I was so lost just looking at her that I didn't see me coming. I emptied myself into her mouth.

I think I got too satisfied that evening and started avoiding her. A week later, she dumped me.

It was too late by the time I realized what a schmuck I'd been. Everybody has weaknesses and strengths. I should have explored other possibilities of enjoying her juicy body. Instead, I tried to set her up with two of my friends.

8

Mid-March. One Sunday at church, I met this kind couple, Pam and David. We got talking and they invited me to their place for dinner. They taught English at many places in and around Angers, including the Chamber of Commerce. They said I should get an English teaching job at the CCI. I said I couldn't teach English, I had never taught before – and what about my Indian accent? But Pam was confident I could get a job at the CCI and said she would talk to somebody there.

And sure enough, she arranged an interview for me, and I got a job as multimedia assistant at Espace Langues, the language teaching section of the CCI. It was a couple of hours in the morning, three days a week, and all I had to do was be there first thing in the morning, open the doors to the computer room for the trainees, see that everything was clean and functioning, and signal any problems to my boss, Sanjay Kakkar, number two at Espace Langues after Roger Mann, an Englishman with an imposing frame and a bald head. I began work on March 12 and for the next five months I lived a sort of double life where I worked mornings at the CCI wearing a tweed jacket and good shoes, and in the afternoon, delivered chicken on a ridiculous little mobilette. I quite enjoyed the experience, really – the money was okay with the two jobs, I often went for lunch at the uni restaurant across the street from the CCI. On my days off, I'd go sit at Bar du Centre with a book and check out the girls.

It was around this time that I met a charming Hungarian honey who went by the name of Paula. I came across her through the student association, Birds of a Feather. She had a quiet, mysterious charm that drew me to her at once. She was staying at the university hostel and gave me her room number, in case I wanted to call her on the common phone in the corridor. She didn't have a mobile. I don't know why no emails were exchanged. I didn't call but sent her a letter. Yes, an actual on-paper letter, asking her to meet me at Ralliement on a certain day and time. She got it too late and called me the next day to apologize. We fixed another day for tea at my place. In those days, Indian tea used to be my most effective bait to lure girls into my room. She came. I made tea and we talked. It was an ideal setting for seduction, the lights were low and we sat on the old wooden floor sipping tea, and we were the only souls in the house. But once again I failed to be proactive. I didn't know what to do.

She had come to my place all alone, and it wasn't because she liked tea. All I had to do was walk up behind her, hold her by the shoulders and kiss her neck. But I think I liked her so much that I wanted to take it slow. So we just talked for a few hours, and then I accompanied her to the bus stop. I never got a second chance to try anything with her. You miss an opportunity and then life takes over, she's busy or you're busy or the time isn't right; and when you finally see her again you don't feel the same intensity or she doesn't show the same interest... or some such deal dampener. The first time is the best time. My little red notebook says that on March 28, I arrived at the CCI fourteen minutes early, went into the toilet and did some creative visualization about Paula's lips, letting the frustration shoot out of my system.

Speaking of toilets, that's another great thing about living in France. There are clean toilets everywhere. In libraries, schools, university campuses, historical monuments, highway rest stops, parking lots and wherever else toilets are supposed to be. French toilets come with a generous supply of toilet paper and thoughtful features like hooks, soap, napkins and hand dryers. It's toilet paradise when you've seen the lack of public facilities in India. On the other hand, the French do not seem to attach much importance to clean drinking water. There are no separate taps for the purpose of drinking. You're supposed to drink from the same taps where you wash your hands after relieving yourself. Yuck.

Anyway, the CCI toilets were clean and smelled good, and the lighting was low. I felt comfortable enough to indulge in an occasional quickie with myself. The same day, as I was about to leave after work, Roger Mann came into sight and asked if I had a minute. I thought he was going to tell me off for wanking in the toilet.

'Just yesterday, Sanjay and I were talking about how you are so western, I mean in your interests and outlook. You like the blues and American poetry,' Roger said. We had talked about all that in my interview. I wondered where this was going. He continued, 'I'm afraid the director of human resources has expressed concern over your wearing the turban at work. She is worried about how far we can go in allowing CCI employees sartorial liberty. If today we allow somebody with a turban, tomorrow we may have to allow somebody with a veil. How do you feel about this?'

'I think it's ridiculous, this whole thing. The turban is not a religious symbol but a part of my personal attire, just like a shirt,' I replied. 'Besides, it's there to hold my long hair in place, and it doesn't hide my face.'

It was absurd. I would understand if they fired me for being incompetent or something, but firing me because I wore a turban was like firing me for wearing a hat to work. Roger was very sympathetic and embarrassed about the whole thing, but he chose his words carefully and said he would see what could be done to resolve the issue. Why the fuck was this woman trying to extend the veil controversy to the turban!

When I told Rémi, he was outraged. 'Don't let those racist motherfuckers have their way, brother,' he said warmly. Roger called the next day and asked me to write a letter to the director of Espace Langues, telling him that I was surprised by this decision and would like to know the precise reasons behind it.

So, with Rémi's help, I wrote a letter and sent it to the CCI. It asked a basic question: what was the problem with my wearing a turban when it had no bearing at all on my work? By next week, all my colleagues knew about it and sympathized. Penny, one of the trainers, said it was a clear case of discrimination at work and I could kick up a stink if they fired me. Roger Mann called me a few days later and said they were not going to fire me. Life returned to normal. Jobs, uni, cafés, sexual starvation, casual masturbation.

By spring, I was quite frustrated about my sexual situation. It's that time of year when hemlines go higher, legs become longer and girls wear dresses the sun comes shining through. And the curves make you salivate endlessly. If you're not getting any in April, you're in a 'water, water everywhere' kind of situation and feel like you're the only one suffering.

I sought consolation in the blues. I listened intensely to Robert Johnson, and it got under my skin, the high moaning voice, the sexual innuendo and the lemon squeezing stuff.

No squeezing was happening to my lemon, and I had to do something about my blues. After some reflection, I went out and bought a basic plastic comb blues harp and an instruction book. I tried playing the tunes in the book but that wasn't quite my thing so I just concentrated on improvising and playing riffs of my own device. I practised all the time, in my room and on the street. I walked around all day, just like Robert Johnson. Walking helped me vent my frustration. One night I was so blue, I walked, blowing the harp, from my place to the other end of rue St Leonard at the other end of town. The harp was also a way of attracting Colline's attention. With Paula gone and no one else in sight, I only had Colline to turn to for an object of desire. She heard me play of course, but I hardly ever saw her.

A week later, I was walking down rue St Aubin, à la Robert de Niro in *Taxi Driver*, feeling blue and lonesome, when I heard a saxophone bebopping. The sound was coming from Le Cool café, where a combo of sax, bass, drums and trombone was playing. I walked in, ordered a beer and sat at a table very close to the musicians. That was my first live jazz gig in France, and it was a good one. I chatted with the musicians later. Yves, the sax player, said he often played at Café du Jour.

I hadn't seen Rémi for some time when I ran into him on the bus that day. He had started dating Pauline recently, and had had a change of attitude. And to think it was my five-kiss trick – you know, four on the cheek, one on the mouth – that had paved his path to Pauline's panties. Had it not been for me, he would still be spanking that monkey.

But rather than becoming my slave out of gratitude, he had become distant and less available. Anyway, we went for a drink and he confessed that he had been keeping a distance because he felt that I had been using him, that every time I called him it was because I needed his help to write a letter in French, or some such thing. I thought that was ridiculous, I mean, I did ask him for small favours but that wasn't what our friendship was based on. It was based on our common love for music, literature and chicks. I was disappointed. I had trusted him completely and it hurt to be misunderstood. I was a foreigner in his country, far away from my family. So what if he helped me in need, that's what friends do. I'd do the same for him. Later, though, I realized I had indeed been asking too many favours of him. Little ones, but far too often. And before Rémi, there were others whom I had asked for help too frequently. I did not realize it could make me look bad and make people want to stay away from me. A lesson learnt. I'm a different man today. I rarely ask people for favours, and when I do I am subtle.

9

Hemming arrived in Angers on April 15. A sad lowdown letter I had written to him in the beginning of the year had inspired him to come down from Copenhagen to lift my spirits. We had met at my boarding school in Chandigarh. Hemming was an exchange student. I had been immediately attracted to the tall, blond, blue-eyed foreigner from the other world, a world that was more hip, glamorous and carefree than the world I lived in. We became friends over a shared love for the Beatles and Elvis. His host family lived in a posh neighbourhood in Chandigarh. I used to rent a room in Mohali. Hemming would bicycle down to my place, we'd go to the roof and he'd do a mean 'Hound Dog' performance. We often went for walks and chai and jalebi. Before he left Chandigarh, he gave me the wonderful Beatles' *White Album*. I didn't dig it at first but it grew on me. 'Why Don't We Do It in the Road?'

I took two days off from the chicken run to entertain my friend. On Monday afternoon, we were at the Civette when dad called. The conversation upset me a little. He started off with the usual questions about how I was doing, what I was doing, what I had planned for the future and how I intended to earn a decent living. I had no answers and it made me feel bad. I told Hemming I felt guilty about not doing anything that could be of any significance to my parents. I wasn't making any money, I had to pay back my loan to mama, I didn't have a respectable job and I was making no progress. Hemming understood what I was going through and said I was doing all right. He himself had spent four years travelling instead of going to school, and he was lagging in terms of qualifications and career, but it didn't matter, he was doing what he wanted to do, and I was doing the same. I was where I had wanted to be, I was living a life I wanted to live and was trying to take it further. I'd find a way. We also had conversations about Kierkegaard, Sartre, Camus and Ayn Rand.

My landlady, who was in the house that week, was not too pleased about my having an overnight guest. One morning she ran into Hemming coming down the stairs, and started ranting to him in French about the extra consumption of electricity and water that his presence caused. I rushed down the stairs to tell her my friend didn't speak any French and that he was leaving on Thursday. That seemed to calm her down a little. Now, how petty can you get? Anybody in their right mind would have spoken to me, not to my guest. Besides, I had one room and I doubted that the light bulb used more electricity if it sensed an extra presence. As for water, so what if there were two or three extra showers that week?

On Wednesday, Hemming and I went bar-hopping and ran into Rémi and his guitar player friend, Pierre. We went to a couple of bars, then came back to my place and talked until late. I would have loved to introduce Hemming to Colline but she wasn't in Angers then. Hemming left on Thursday.

Life went on prosaically, amidst two jobs and afternoons at the American library reading self-help books like *Think and Grow Rich* and *15 Steps to Impossible Dreams*. The library was my haven. I read there, took naps and also discovered new faces. In the evenings, I went to Bar du Centre for drinks with a gang of German students I had met at uni. We talked about women and they taught me useful phrases in German. *Fahne drube und furs faterland* is German for 'Cover the face and do it for the fatherland'. Maja, a promiscuous German beauty, hung out with us once in a while. She liked me and I sort of fell in love with her. More fool I. Aside from her full ass, I loved the sound of her voice and the shape of her mouth when she said *ja* or *sheisse*. One evening, at Café du Jour, Maja and I were talking dirty and she was telling me how her previous boyfriend's cock was painfully big for her and how perfect her current boyfriend's tool was and how she liked plenty of foreplay and how she loved it from behind. I said, '*Ich gerne dich werne kussen.*' I would like to kiss you. She said something in German that I didn't understand but I leaned forward and laid a wet one on her mouth. She responded.

Halfway through the kiss, I drew away. Her boyfriend was close by. Then somebody said something, something happened and she had to leave in a hurry. There were other occasions when she kissed me on the mouth, her lips fully pressed against mine. She was bisexual and had an open relationship with her boyfriend. I guess I could have arranged for Maja and me to be in the same sack. If I hadn't been a dimwit loser, that is. I lacked confidence and was too slow to do anything productive. Or maybe it just wasn't meant to be.

There were several similar situations with other girls where my mojo failed. Nothing to write home about.

Speaking of home, I didn't really keep in touch with my parents during this time. In part, because phoning from the telephone booths was expensive. Also, because I didn't know what to tell them about what I was doing and how I planned to be somebody. Becoming somebody has always been a big thing with me. I don't know how I acquired that notion but the thought of living life as a common chump irks me. My grandfather used to say that I would become an important person, a bada aadmi. I think my subconscious took it too seriously. And here I was, years later, a common chump who couldn't even get laid.

10

One sunny Sunday, I went to church after a long time. My morning shifts at the chicken run had kept me from Mass for weeks. That day I met Thomas, an Englishman studying theology in France. In the course of our conversation he told me that he relied on God for everything.

'God is the boss. He knows what makes me happy, he knows what makes me boogie, and he takes me wherever I'm going to be happy. I get on the boat and God steers it. There are times when the sea gets too rough, I'm afraid the waves are too high and violent. I'm so scared, I don't wanna go any further. I say to him, God, I don't wanna go any further. I'd be all right where I was. And God says, Thomas, who's the boss here? I say, It's you, God. And he tells me not to be afraid, and he gets me there safe. We reach the shore, I find my happiness. There are things to do. The weather gets bad or the boat needs attention, you know, but everything is taken care of with God's help.'

I walked back home wondering when my boat was going to hit the shore. I wasn't getting anywhere in life. Or love.

Then one morning in late May, I woke up like never before, or after. I opened my eyes and lay in bed and felt in a state of perfect equilibrium. That must be what they call zen. I was neither happy nor sad, neither excited nor down. Usually, I woke up in the morning with depressing thoughts. But that day I felt calm. No worries, no anxiety, a state that can supposedly be achieved by meditation. It's never happened to me again.

I went to the supermarket to change the empty gas cylinder, and came back to find Anne-Sophie and her parents waiting for me at the door. Anne-Sophie had been my neighbour at the students' hostel. I didn't recognize her for a second. She was a friend but we had never been that close or anything. I never thought she would pay me a visit. She was still at Cuffon Pavot, and in the second year at the Catho. Apparently she had spoken about me to her parents, so when they came to fetch her for the weekend they decided to pay me a visit. A nice surprise, and it made me feel even better on that zen day. I offered them tea and prunes and they invited me to visit them in the countryside near Nantes.

Sylvie, the manager at the chicken job, told me about this blues festival in Cognac that she was going to volunteer at in July. I decided to go too, and quit the chicken job. I had had enough of it. The Blues Passion Festival took place in the main park in Cognac. There were three big stages in three corners of the park and several small stages in the middle. Most of the volunteers were young people. There was a makeshift restaurant in the middle of the park where all the volunteers got together for meals. It was a nice atmosphere of carefree camaraderie. I was in charge of the main stage, for the most famous artists. I met some of the biggest names in blues: Keb Mo, Canned Heat, Alvin Youngblood Heart and others. I also met a couple of gorgeous volunteers, Julie and Lucille. They were about twenty-one–twenty-two. I fell for Lucille: blonde, beautiful, cute and sexy. She saw my interest and started playing with me, that devil in disguise. On the last evening of the festival, after the final concert, as we were having a drink, she came and sat in my lap. I put my arm around her waist and caressed her semi-bare back. Seemed I wouldn't have to go to bed alone that night. Later in the evening, I walked up to Lucille at one point and took her in my arms. She shrugged off my embrace and said I was being too brash. For the rest of the evening she remained cold and distant, and it became clear that all she had intended was to tease me. The next morning at the Cognac station, while waiting for my train back to Angers, I broke down and cried. I had fallen for that cockteasing bitch. And you must understand, it wasn't just she that caused me to cry, it was the weight of this poor wretched life, the frustration of not getting anywhere and not knowing what to do. Lucille was just the last straw that made me feel like a complete failure.

What did I learn from it? Well, I've learnt to take the teasing in my stride and enjoy it like a game. You've got to be strong in the head and not get your hopes too high nor get emotionally attached. When a mischievous woman senses the sucker in you, she deploys all her cunning to pull you deep into the trap, only to leave you in the lurch and make you suffer for the sin of having given into temptation. Women are like carnivorous plants. I think it makes them feel powerful. And sex is all about power. Be strong and you won't go wrong.

On my return journey from Cognac, I made a two-day stopover at Anne-Sophie's parents' home. Her dad really liked me. He dug my rudimentary harp playing and praised my French to embarrassment. And I realized that I didn't know Anne-Sophie at all. I didn't know if she had a boyfriend, or if she was a lesbian. I would have loved to get to know her better, but she remained aloof.

I had been in Angers a couple of days when Julie, from the blues festival, called and invited me to her parents' house in the countryside near Cognac. She had witnessed the Lucille fiasco and wanted to hook me up with one of her girlfriends whom she had invited for the weekend. In those days I welcomed every opportunity, even one that required me to take the train back to the south-west of France.

Julie revealed the bitter truth about Lucille. She had a boyfriend, a forty-two-year-old man with kids. She had been playing me all along. You know, women love my attentions.

The first night at Julie's place, we went to a nightclub. The bouncer at the door told me to take off my turban if I wanted to get in. Some clubs in France had a policy of not letting in people with hats. A long argument followed, and it took us forty minutes to convince the guy to let me in. Julie and her friends danced, I sat around. It wasn't fun. We got back in the wee hours of the morning and a gloom descended over me again. That evening, I took the train back to Angers. I didn't hook up with any of Julie's friends. It was an uneventful trip, except for the turban trouble. Towards the end of July, my brother Samar informed me that he was in Sydney, where he had enrolled in an MBA programme. I was amazed at the sheer speed at which this had happened. I didn't even know he had any such plans. That moment on, I felt very proud telling people my brother studied business in Sydney. People usually said, 'You're a family of globetrotters!'

I left for Denmark on August 16. Somewhere between Hemming's departure and Cognac, I had made plans to visit Hemming and his family. It was a seventeen-hour bus ride on Eurolines and then a ferry to get to Copenhagen from Angers. Hemming met me at the station and we took the train to Nykobing on the island of Falster, where his parents lived. From the Nykobing station, we headed straight to the main city square, Hemming carrying my rucksack as if it were a child's schoolbag. A band was playing traditional music and his parents were at a bar drinking beer. Hemming handed me a huge glass of beer. I looked at it, wondering if I'd ever finish it.

'Welcome to Denmark!' said Hemming, clearly amused by my dilemma.

When I met Hemming's parents, I finally understood why my Danish friend was such a gentle, soft-spoken fellow.

His father, an electrical engineer, was a cheerful, charming man; his mother was lovely, she spoke little English and was a fantastic cook. His eldest brother Pontus lived in the countryside near Copenhagen with his wife and two children. The middle brother Jens was a long-haired adventuresome intellectual. He was going out with a Swedish girl he had met at the Roskilde music festival. They were all really tall.

I had a very good time in Nykobing. Delicious food, stimulating conversation, fabulous wine and Gammel Dansk, a Danish bitters – *the* Danish bitters, in fact. It's served in small glasses and is suitable for every occasion throughout the day, starting with breakfast. Hemming said when he was in school, he and his friends would go to class drunk on Gammel Dansk.

We went to Copenhagen after that, and visited the Viking museum in Roskilde on our way. I learnt that the Vikings subjected their enemies to slow impalement and drank their blood straight from the skulls. *Skoll!*

We strolled through the cobbled pedestrian streets of Copenhagen talking, eating and ogling at tall, beautiful women biking past in short flowing skirts. Well, I ogled while Hemming played discreet behind his dark Ray-Bans. After a long sabbatical, travelling and trying to figure out what he wanted to do in life, Hemming had decided to go back to school and become a librarian. It was a five-year degree. The library system in Denmark is very well organized and all the libraries in the country are part of one nationwide network and share databases and resources. If you are in Copenhagen you can request a document from a library in the other side of the country and check it out at the local library when it arrives. The librarians are skilled managers and technicians, hence the long years of study and training.

Because it was extremely hard to find an apartment in Copenhagen, Hemming had reserved a room in somebody's apartment and had already been paying rent for two months, intending to move in when school started. But now for some reason the landlord said the room wasn't available any more. Hemming and I went to see him to find out if the guy was going to give Hemming his money back. I didn't like his face, he looked wicked. Hemming spoke to him in Danish. When we came out on the street, Hemming told me he was not getting his money back. I was furious and started cursing the guy, calling him a black motherfucker who should be put in jail for fraud.

'Not because he's black,' said Hemming, embarrassed. 'Blacks were the original jazzmen, remember.'

'Yeah, whatever, these guys are the cause of all the trouble in France.' I don't know where that came from. Maybe I had seen black guys make trouble. It was an obvious lack of culture and experience.

Hemming looked pensive and handsome in his short-sleeved shirt and dark glasses. As we walked past the museum of erotica, in the middle of downtown Copenhagen, I said, 'Hey, let's go in there. What do you think?'

'Right now, I'm just thinking one thing,' said Hemming, looking straight ahead.

'And what is that?'

'How to find a pussy with a room.'

That cracked me up. I saw Hemming's sombre Ray-Banned face gazing into the distance, saying 'pussy with a room' against the backdrop of the erotic museum. I think it was the only time I heard him say pussy.

We went out with his friends, his erstwhile girlfriend and her beautiful friend Julianne. Jacob, a good-looking medical student-cum-surfer, took us to his flat and insisted on showing us a Danish porn movie by Lars Braun. He said I would like it because it was aesthetic porn. It turned out to be the usual porn fare. He made us some Irish coffee, which wasn't very good either. I had a good time in Copenhagen, even though no little mermaid floated up my way. The evening I was to leave, Hemming and I caught a swinging hard-bop gig at Studentehusset and he gave me a copy of *The Way to Danish*, to help me improve my Danish. It was hard saying goodbye.

At the end of summer, they gave me a few more hours at the CCI. The salary was about 2000 francs, which was quite enough to survive and pay for drinks at that time. Life continued as it had before the summer: CCI job, cafés, having no sex and worrying about the future. I identified more and more with Kerouac's tortured soul, his love for jazz, his frustration about not fulfilling his quest for wealth and glory, and most importantly, the fact that he had a mother he wanted to make comfortable. I felt a brotherly love towards him. I wished he had known how to handle his celebrity. I was cross with Capote for making fun of him and I had a bone to pick with Brando for not responding to his letter.

I joined Fous de Jazz, an association that organized jazz concerts in Angers. A few months earlier, I had sent them a letter asking to join the association. The president of the association, Gaëton, phoned and invited me for a concert, where I made acquaintance with him and the other members. They tacitly accepted me as a member. All I had to do was help them set up and remove the equipment and chairs before and after the concerts, and attend weekly meetings.

And I got to attend all the concerts for free, which was one of the reasons why I had wanted to join the association in the first place.

At one of the meetings, I suggested we expand the association to include university students. They liked the idea and we did a promo offering one ticket for two students. Some students came, but just that once. The idea of college kids digging jazz belonged only in movies set in the '60s.

As an active member of the association, I also had the unspoken privilege of inviting a friend from time to time. Once I invited a girl from the church, Angeline, a discreet cutie, slim and tall. It was my first live gig of avant-garde jazz, the Michel Edelin and François Méchali duo. In those days, I didn't dig that stuff. It didn't swing, it didn't bop. But my church friend liked it. Though we appreciated each other, nothing happened between Angeline and me. She never showed more than friendly interest and I didn't try anything. Nothing ever happened between me and any of the church girls, in fact. All the girls my age were taken except Angeline and Lucy, the pastor's daughter. She had really big breasts, I mean, they were gorgeous. She had golden hair, a splendid ass and the face of an angel. She always gave me the impression that she would have been a bad, bad broad if she weren't the pastor's daughter. I could see a sea of mischief simmering under her good-girl face.

September. To make some extra dough, I took up a one-day inventory-making job at Leroy Merlin, the DIY megastore. All I had to do was count the merchandise one by one, shelf by shelf, and put up a Post-it with the quantity of the item. There were other young people there, each worked independently in his or her assigned row. I saw one delicious babe but didn't get a chance to talk to her. I was one of the last to finish. At the end of the day, I exited the store through the back and I got talking with this black girl who had just finished as well. She smiled first. She was not that good-looking, but tall and slim. Normally I wouldn't pay much attention to her, but I had already been DIYing since before Denmark.

'*Salut*, do I know you?' I enquired with a smile.

She nodded. 'I have seen you around at the university,' she said in a lilting voice.

'Oh, yeah? What do you study? Are you taking the bus?'

She was taking the bus all right. We talked on the bus and I decided to invite her over to my place. As the bus approached my stop, I asked if she'd like to come in for a cuppa, she hesitated for a moment but agreed. We got off, went up to my room and I made tea. We talked about India, the turban and all that 'exotic guy' jazz. The conversation wasn't going anywhere. As a rule, when a girl you've just met comes over, it's because she likes you and more or less expects something to happen between the two of you. There's tension in all your extremities. But here there was no tension. She wasn't thinking about it at all. She was innocent, naïve, inexperienced. It was my responsibility to get on with it.

She sat on the edge of the small bed. In the middle of our conversation, I stood beside her and started playing with her braided hair. Then I lay down on the bed behind her and expressed my desire to give her a massage. She shook her head. Then I proceeded to kiss her. She pulled away.

'Why are you doing this?' she said. 'Because I came up to your place, you think I'll sleep with you?'

'No, I'm doing this because I like you. That's why I asked you to come up in the first place.'

She sat on the side of the bed with her thighs glued together in defensive tension. I lay there, held her right hand and began to rant languorously about how beautiful she was and how wonderful it would be if we were together, gradually drawing my body closer to hers. By the time my cheek was against her right thigh, I felt the tension in her arms and legs ease. My mojo was working for once. Her legs relaxed, and my hand slid across her thigh. I kissed her over her jeans. Then I lifted my head and saw her face full of longing, and kissed her. We kissed for about thirty seconds and she thrust her tongue into my mouth.

That was the fastest seduction I have ever achieved. The lesson here is this: to seduce a woman, you gotta talk to her, say the things she wants to hear, capture her imagination, induce in her the feelings that lead to desire. I hadn't planned anything, I just followed my instinct and the words, combined with a little physical contact, did it. We kissed and talked. She asked me if I had slept with many women before. Any girl you sleep with will ask you that! I told her the truth: 'Just a few.' That's the truth, I'm no Casanova, though I wish I were. I would certainly have done better, made a greater score if I hadn't been an arrogant loner type and had learnt the value of cherishing sex as it came.

After a lot of kissing and promises, I escorted her to her studio at Ralliement and I went to see her again the next evening. She was in the middle of dinner. I lay in her bed and waited for her to finish eating. I invited her to come lie with me. She asked me what we were going to do. I said we would lie in bed together and see where it went. She lay next to me, still wearing her woollen sweater. It felt rough, and I have pretty sensitive skin. But when I asked her to take it off, she refused. I tried to feel her breasts, she pushed me away. I tried to slide my hand into her jeans but she stopped me. At the same time, she kept talking sentimental crap.

'Tell me I'm beautiful.'

I didn't want to tell her that because I didn't find her beautiful, but I said it anyway.

As I said before, too much talk and no action makes me a very unhappy boy. *Acta non verba* is the way to go if you wanna get along with me. But I was a fool, she only wanted me to turn her on with talk. I asked her again to take off the sweater and change into something softer. She shook her head stubbornly. That was the last straw. All I wanted from her was some foreplay, ejaculation and some sleep, 'coz I had to go to work early next morning. I had no energy for this drama. 'Fuck you!' I said and got out of bed and put on my shoes. 'I'm done.'

She looked shocked. 'Why?' she asked.

'Because you are stubborn and insensitive,' I snapped.

She said she was afraid, it was her first time. I said I didn't want anything to do with her any more. She asked if we could be friends, I said no. Then she got angry and screamed at me. I left.

Once again, folks, impatience and arrogance got me out of a box before I could climb into it. I spotted her in the street a couple of months later, she had filled out and looked really juicy, with a nice, round ass, and I couldn't help feeling a tinge of regret. I had robbed myself of the noble deed of initiating a nubile one on the path of pleasure. I could have been patient and tried to make her comfortable. It was her first time and she had the right to be apprehensive. Instead of being an intelligent, sensitive lover, I was an impatient asshole, bent on instant gratification. I could have been her mentor and taught her the joys of sex and how to use her mouth more creatively. But I ruined it all.

11

On the afternoon of September 11, I strolled into the city centre and ran into Anne-Lise having a drink outside a café. She asked if I had heard the news. I hadn't. The World Trade Centre in New York had fallen. Two airplanes had rammed into the Twin Towers. A band of Arabs had actually blown up New York. Just like Kerouac wrote in *On the Road*!

Somehow, maybe because I was too preoccupied with my own internal turmoil, the gravity of the event did not register. It would have, if I had a TV at home. The next day I noticed people staring at me a little more than they did before. The day after, I saw an old woman look alarmed when she walked past me. At a news-stand, I came face to face with Osama bin Laden's bearded, turbaned face on the cover of a magazine. The headline said something about the face of terrorism. At that moment I realized why people were looking at me as if I was some kind of spectre. I was the only person in Angers who bore any likeness to the Islamist lunatics.

Before 9/11, older women would look at me with curiosity and often smile at me. After 9/11, they looked in horror and hastened home. One time I was walking down the street with a girl when an Arab guy on the other side of the street stared at me with an unpleasant expression. God knows why. A few days later, I went to a bar with Rémi and Pierre, and a young guy who had had one too many said, '*Salut Taliban!*' I told him he didn't know what the fuck he was saying, I was a Sikh and I came from India. He apologized but we left the bar soon after. When we were outside, Pierre said there had been another guy in the bar who had called me bin Laden under his breath.

At the CCI, I didn't notice anything different. It was on my way to work that people stared at me. I normally walked to the CCI, but on this particular day I took the bus. I leaned against a pole in the middle of the bus and started reading. It was Sexus, if I remember right. Halfway to my stop, I had an uneasy feeling that forced me to look up. As I did, I found every single passenger in the bus staring at me, their eyes digging into my skin. I wanted to cry out, 'What the fuck are you looking at, you ignorant frogs? I come from India and I'm a Sikh. Sikhs wear turbans. And all I care about is women, wine and jazz.' Of course, I didn't say anything, just pretended to read in indifference. Never took that bus again.

Only two days later, I was walking down the street when a kid behind me shouted, 'Bin Laden!' I spun around on my heels, face burning with rage, ready to hit. It was just a little boy. He shrank back in fear. After staring at him for five seconds, I turned and continued walking, still burning.

It was becoming increasingly difficult for me to go out without feeling embarrassed, even going to eat at the university restaurant was unpleasant. Everybody stared. The thought of forsaking the turban did cross my mind, but I didn't want to give up my identity just because the frogs couldn't distinguish between the Taliban turban and a Sikh turban. Nevertheless, I did avoid eye contact with people and stopped going to bars.

One late October evening, my colleague from the CCI, Will Pearson, persuaded me to go to an Irish pub in rue Chateau Gontier. I didn't really want to but he pushed me. I relented and we joined Don and Laurie, also from the CCI, at the pub. I sat there not saying much, moping by myself. When I said I wanted to leave, Will took me outside and gave me a pep talk. We came back inside and had another drink. A long-haired, crocodile dundee type guy started talking to us in English – he introduced himself as Tony Marsh, from fish town Grimsby in northern England. He was a rose-grafter and had recently moved to Angers with his French girlfriend. Tony told us a bit about his work and that it involved a lot of travelling across Europe.

'That sounds so Beat,' I said.

'Yeah, mate, I am Beat. I'm a bluesman,' Tony said, brandishing his harp.

'Wow, could you play something?'

He played some blues riffs. I was seriously impressed and invited him to play at the Beat poetry evening I was organizing at the American library in December. I asked him if he would teach me to play the harp. He agreed and said he normally got paid for this but I could just buy him beer. By the time the bar was closing, Laurie was drunk and didn't want to leave. When the barman insisted we leave, Laurie in turn insisted that he listen to Tony's blues, '*Écoutez, écoutez!*' he cried. 'Listen!'

Tony made me buy a Marine Band harp and started to give me lessons. Twice a week, once at my place, once at his. Tony and his girlfriend Laureline lived in a tiny studio behind the railway station. Laureline was about twenty-three, Tony was forty. Both of them liked to smoke grass and drink wine. On more than one occasion, I stayed for dinner. Tony would fix us good, simple food, with coleslaw, potatoes and eggs. I liked to eat with them. We talked about life, the blues, the Beats, money and work.

Tony was a funny guy. We joked about him adopting me so that I could live and work freely in Europe. Once we went out for drinks with Laureline's friends, and Tony whispered to Laureline and me, 'Don't bother to pay when we leave.' Her friends had to fork it out for us. Another time, we were about to go out and Tony couldn't find his hairbrush. So you know what he did? He brushed his long hair with a toothbrush!

One evening, after harp practice and dinner, the three of us went to Saltimbanque, a bar in the little street near 400 Coups. They had an open mic and there were groups of young people who took turns singing on stage. There were three girls at a table in front of us. They were good-looking and had full, lusty bodies, with slim waists and wide behinds straight out of Peter Fendi's 'Gentlemen Callers'. Just the thought of them is making me randy right now.

Finally these three girls went on stage together and sang something funny. As they climbed off the stage and made their way back to their table, Tony said something to the most attractive one. He spoke in English. He was quite drunk by this time and spoke slowly in a low voice. He asked her where she came from, she said she and her friends were from Rennes, he said he was a rose-grafter. When the girl sat down, Tony began to flirt more openly, complimenting her looks, and then he asked her to come back to his place. I was shocked – not to mention embarrassed! Picture it: I am sitting on Tony's right, the girl's sitting on his left, Laureline is sitting across the table. And here was Tony asking this girl to go home with him right under his girlfriend's nose. Laureline pretended not to pay attention and just looked towards the stage. The girl resisted, Tony insisted.

'Why do you want me to come with you? What will you do if I come with you?' she asked, as if looking for a valid reason to go home with him.

Tony looked at her, licked his lips and said, 'I'll take you home, then I'll kiss your neck... I'll take your shirt off, then I'll lick your boobs...'

'What's boobs?' she asked. Tony gestured, she got it.

'I'll kiss your stomach... then I'm gonna rip off your panties...' He bit his lip. The girl was visualizing the scenario. I could see it in her face. When Tony was done laying out the business plan, she said he was not a gentleman and went back to her table. Then the three of us left the bar and went back to Tony's place.

The next morning, Tony remembered what had transpired only vaguely, or maybe he was just pretending to forget, and laughed it off. Laureline didn't make a fuss. She seemed to understand that he had been too drunk to know what he was doing. I had felt embarrassed at the bar, but later I realized that what Tony did that night was a great seduction technique which you will find in any good book on the subject, that is, inducing in a woman the desire for sex by painting word pictures, delivered with the right body language, emotion and voice. From the expression on the girl's face I could see that Tony had got her imagination working and she was feeling an attraction for him. His words, as they came out of his lascivious lips, had sent her into a light trance which would have become stronger had she allowed him to continue with the word-painting.

Why she didn't agree to go home with him is beside the point, because even if she had agreed, Laureline would not have let her. The girl must have sensed this potential obstacle, or maybe she didn't want to be separated from her friends. A woman can have a hundred reasons not to fuck a stranger on a particular night, even if she wants to. The point is, he made her want to.

Tony was a natural. When we were just the two of us, he would tell me about all the women he had had in different countries in Europe. He was a champion player, never without a woman for too long. Always shacking up with the next available broad that crossed his path. I thought his life, his conquests and boisterous personality would make a fascinating book.

In November, they closed the multimedia assistant position at the CCI and I was out of a job. Looking back now, they might have done it just to get rid of me in the wake of 9/11, more efficiently this time. I dedicated myself completely to organizing the Beat evening at the American library, got in touch with two Beat scholars in Angers. One of them lent me some cassette tapes of Jack Kerouac reading his poetry with jazz. I decided to do something on the same lines and got in touch with Yves, the sax player. I had no sense of music and had never considered myself a performer. I was not sure if I could pull it off, but I had to give it a try. Yves was interested and said we'd get together one of these days and rehearse. In the meantime, I practised alone, reading Kerouac's haikus aloud, imitating his tone. I organized the entire event almost single-handedly, made posters, put them up at various places, and invited all kinds of people. All this running around greatly helped keep my mind off the fact that people stared at me, and being in charge of things kept me from completely losing morale. Thanks to a journalist friend, my picture even appeared in *Courrier de l'Ouest*, announcing the event.

The Beat evening went beautifully. I started it off with a welcome poem I had written. The two Beat scholars read Kerouac's haikus and Gary Snyder poems. Rémi and some others read in French, Tony sang some blues. I read a couple of Kerouac haikus, with Yves improvising on tenor sax.

A few days before Christmas, my friend Nicolas said he and his friend were going to Spain for the New Year's, and could take me along if there was enough room in the car. I celebrated Christmas at Gilles's mother's place with his nephews. Then I began to plan for the trip to Spain. I was worried that I was going to scare the Spaniards. If they saw a bearded guy with a turban at the party, they'd freak out. I didn't want the stares on New Year's Eve. So I tried a few things and found a way of tying my hair in a little bun at the back of my head, without the turban. It looked okay. The skin between the forehead and the hairline was distinctly paler than the rest of me, but what the heck. A few days later, Nicolas called and said I was not going to Spain, because there was no room in the car.

'Fuck!' I said but I didn't feel so bad, I was excited about my new look. I could have put the turban back on and continued with life as before, but I decided to keep the new me. I felt light and free. This was the freedom I had desired as a teenager in school. I grew up wishing I could look like the regular guys who didn't have to wear a turban and were allowed to shave. Girls in India were attracted to clean-shaven guys. But of course I didn't have the balls to go get my hair cut for fear that my family would disown me, or weep and cry, and make me feel bad about bringing dishonour upon them.

I celebrated New Year's Eve in the countryside, at the house of a friend's friend near Fontainebleau. I knew nobody there. It shattered my vain belief that I had the ability to make friends and have fun with strangers anywhere. That night, I realized this ability depended heavily on the inclination of strangers to be friends with me, and in Fontainebleau they didn't give a fuck. Nobody tried to talk to me or make me comfortable. They all knew each other and had a good time, I had a terrible time. I swore never again to find myself in the company of people I didn't know on New Year's Eve. It's better to be alone and read a book than to be with strangers and watch them smear Nutella on each other's faces, while you sit on the sofa pretending to be amused.

2002

12

How long was the longest period you didn't fuck? I hadn't had it since time immemorial. My little red rooster was so blue it had to be consoled three to four times a week. I didn't have a job, either. Further salt on the wound, the Euro kicked in and brought with it a rise in prices. Almost everything that used to cost 5 francs now cost a euro, which was 6.66 francs.

Will Pearson invited me to Nantes to introduce me to his boss at Ecole Centrale, who he said might offer me a job teaching English. Will had moved to Nantes in November last year. He was surprised to see me without my turban. I stayed with him for two days. All we ate were kebabs and burgers. Will wasn't getting laid either. He told me he could see the English department secretary's panties under her desk when he sat at his.

Will was the most fucking jinxed guy I have ever known. Bad things happened to him all the time. Not just small things but real accidents; he was even mugged once. Every month I'd hear of something unfortunate happening to him. He had problems with his employers and changed jobs often. I discovered there were people who didn't want anything to do with Will for fear of having his jinx rub off on them. I loved Will. All the shit that happened to him could never steal his humour. To me, he personified the word debonair with his clever humour, constant smile and suave manner. Once, commenting on his latest accident, I said, 'I should write a book about you. What shall I title it?'

'*Mein Kampf* 2,' fired Will. He had a way of making anything sound funny just by the way he said it. He mentored me and tried to help me find a job, and came down to Angers from time to time for a drink. Don and Laurie often joined us. One evening, Don told me he was in touch with sexy Romanian chicks over the internet, who offered themselves for pleasure and said it was really cheap in Romania.

'Hmm, Romania...Transylvania,' I thought aloud.

'Don't know if you're gonna get your dick sucked, mate, but you'll certainly get your blood sucked,' Will pointed out.

Another time, Will and I were sitting on the steps of the Grand Théatre, contemplating life, ladies, money and the nice clothes it can buy. I said that I didn't really care about clothes any more.

'Yeah, you're more into taking them off.' We laughed and Will went on, 'You know, no woman wants you to whip her knickers down, give her a quick seeing-to and then bye-bye. They want trust, yeah, trust and love. They like to think you're the man they want to go long-term with.'

'Really?'

'Really. You've got to keep the humpy-rumpy under wraps until such a time as she trusts you. When they trust you, you have a good chance at the horizontal dance, not before.'

Later, Will met a nurse in Nantes, thanks to an accident, he had a baby with her and they moved to England. Then they had another baby and moved to a house that was apparently haunted by fun-loving ghosts who created havoc every night. Then Will had an accident at the school where he worked and sued them. Last time I heard from him, he was not working any more, he was walking with a stick and drawing a good invalidity allowance. Life wasn't bad.

I didn't have any luck in Nantes. Came back to Angers and found a job at a small language school. They sent me to give conversation lessons to managers at NEC computers. I began to visit Don frequently. He had quit the CCI, got separated from his French wife and worked at ESMA. I liked Don's company, his laidback demeanour and Californian speech. He introduced me to Bangbus and other cool stuff on the web.

One evening, I was at the Fous de Jazz venue for a concert by the young French pianist, Baptiste Trotignon. I was standing near the make-shift bar talking to somebody when my eyes were drawn to this short-haired redhead who had queued up to buy tickets, she was staring at me. She looked away, then back at me. She seemed nervous. Her lips were quivering and she couldn't take her eyes off me. Clearly, she was smitten. Each time I looked at her, I caught her staring at me. She was with a group of people, among them a guy who maybe she was with, so I didn't go up to her. During the interval, I spotted her sitting two rows behind me. I turned and smiled, she smiled back and the tension eased. After the concert, I looked around and found her standing outside with the same people she had come with. I should have just gone over to the group and said, 'Hi, did you like the gig? I work for Fous de Jazz, I've never seen you guys before.' That might have led to something; at least I would have found out if she was from another city, just visiting friends. But I didn't do that and the girl and her friends left.

For many masturbating months, I consoled myself with the thought that there had been a cute redhead smitten by the mere sight of me.

Despite my irresistible charm, I was still not getting any. Some time went by in rambling, reading, getting bored and harp playing. I could bend notes by now, thanks to Tony's lessons. Colline re-enrolled at the Catho for her CAPES preparation, she did not get through last year. People rarely do. CAPES is tough and you hardly learn anything about teaching, but it does get you a permanent job with the Education Nationale. One late evening in January, I was so overcome with thoughts of Colline that I went downstairs and knocked at her door.

'I'm already in bed,' she called out.

'It's important.'

'Come in then.'

I entered; she was in bed, under a quilt. I kneeled on the floor beside her and said, 'Colline, I love you.' She pointed at a picture at the side table. 'That's David. We've been together six months.'

'It doesn't matter, I just wanted to let you know that I can't stop thinking about you.' I asked her to place her hand on my heart and feel how fast it was beating. She declined. I wished her goodnight and went out of her room. That's the last time I remember seeing her. I think my heart was purged of her that night.

I was still in touch with Birds of a Feather, the students' association. There were quite a few Hungarian chicks in the association this year. I tried to get it on with a couple of them but had no luck. One weekend in March, the association arranged to take the students to Paris for a students' forum. It was a free ride to Paris, and baby, I'm always in for a free ride. The bus left on Saturday morning. I sat next to a slim blonde named Louise and we had a pleasant conversation. She laughed when I told her I had been inspired to come to France by Alain Delon movies. I enjoyed her company. The forum was at La Villette. We arrived past lunchtime and were greeted with a variety of cheeses, breads and wines.

The place was like an indoor fair; each association had its own space with kiosks, and the members presented music and dance performances. Louise and I ran into each other a few times while making rounds of the different performances. We shared a good vibe. When we had some time to spare we went outside and sat by the river Seine. I talked her into letting me give her a shoulder massage. In the evening, Leo Wiplinger said he was going for a jazz performance somewhere in Paris and I could tag along. I asked Louise to come with us and she agreed. During the concert, I pretended to be tired and rested my head on her shoulder. One thing led to another and I held her hand and we kissed. Leo split after the performance, and Louise and I walked all the way back to the Villette. We wandered around Paris the next day, before the bus took us back to Angers. Louise and I exchanged phone numbers. She came to see me the next evening, and we made love. Then on, she came to my place regularly, often staying over. My bed was not large enough for two, so she brought a sleeping bag and left it on the floor. We discovered that we shared the same date of birth. I was two years older. I introduced her to Tony and Laureline.

Tony and I had a serious conversation about my finances. He said I should go rose-grafting with him in Belgium. It was hard work but I could make real money. He worked for six months and made enough to live and buy beer for the rest of the year. He said I could work in Belgium as his friend Nick's assistant. I was thrilled at the prospect of learning a real skill that would allow me to travel around Europe, make money and get laid after work. I agreed, and we began training together to meet the physical demands of the job. I'd run to Tony's place thrice a week in the morning, and he'd make me do push-ups, sit-ups and weights. The weights were one-litre plastic water bottles, stuck together with tape, five bottles for five kilos.

In April, the racist far-right leader, Le Pen, got to the second round of presidential elections and drew international attention. My friend Nicolas sent me an SMS that day, saying: 'I am ashamed of being French.' A lot of people felt that way. If Le Pen became president, I could kiss goodbye to all hopes of a future in France.

I called Nick, and he asked me to send my documents to the Belgian employer: a copy of my passport, social security number, etc. I was supposed to leave mid-June. In the middle of May, Nick called to say there was a problem – I could not work in Belgium because I was not an EU citizen. I said I had a student visa and could work in France full-time during the summer holidays, so I should be able to work in Belgium. I also called the employer to explain. They were sympathetic but said the local labour office had refused to issue me a work permit. I called the Indian embassy, who told me I did have the right to work in Belgium. I called the employer again, then the ministry of foreign affairs in Belgium and a couple of other organizations. My chances looked bleak. But I was not going to give up. I had been training for two months and was ready for the work and the money it would bring. I decided to go with Tony anyway, and see what could be done on the spot.

Tony and I took the train to Rennes and then drove to Belgium with an English couple, husband and wife. They had been rose-grafting for fifteen years. The wife, Sorel, was a beautiful, fragile-looking woman. I wondered how she managed the hardship in the summer heat. The rose fields were somewhere in the Belgian countryside near Ghent. Nick took me to the labour office the very first day, and spoke to the lady in Dutch. She said she could not give me permission to work in Belgium because I was not an EU citizen, and then she disappeared. Apparently she already knew about my case. It was final, I couldn't work in the roses there. Plan B was to go to the ministry of labour in Brussels and try to get a work permit. I left at once.

In Brussels, I stayed with my friend Pierre, the guitar player, who was doing an internship at a music festival. There were other French people in his building, students and trainees, including Fiona, the beautiful, green-eyed, French-Portuguese architecture student. The first evening at Pierre's place, we were all eating in the common kitchen when Fiona entered. She did a two-peck *bonjour* to everybody, and when she did it to me, our lips brushed against each other, accidently but very obviously. Everybody noticed. After dinner, Pierre said, 'You practically pounced upon her, skirt-chaser.' I said it was just my animal magnetism that had pulled her lips to mine.

The next morning, I went to the ministry of labour but the person I met said that the matter should be referred to another department in Ghent. The following day I was in Ghent, but the office had already closed. That night I went out with Pierre and his friends, including Fiona. We went to this very Bohemian place, where there were lots of people and a band playing. There were moments when I felt a spark between me and Fiona, like when she looked at me intently at the bar. But she was just leading me on.

I went back to Ghent the next day. The person in charge was a tall, slim, elegant lady, not yet forty. She expressed sympathy and explained that I, not being a citizen of the EU, really did not have the right to work in Belgium. That put a full stop to my quest. I had already been to all the concerned offices and everyone had said the same thing. I went back to Brussels, disheartened, and stayed there for a few days trying to figure out what to do. I went to the cathedral, sat on a bench and wept. During my week in Brussels, I managed to be disliked by almost everybody, even had a tiff with Pierre. An email from Louise brightened me up a little. Before I left, Pierre showed me the famous red-light district where women of the street sat, or stood, in glass cages and tried to lure the clients with crude gestures. It was a sordid sight. I didn't have a good time in Brussels, nor did I have a good feeling about the city itself.

I came back to Angers, looked for a job, and finally got lucky. I began to work as night receptionist at a small hotel near the Catho. It was a temporary contract for a month and a half to replace a receptionist on sick leave. The night shift was from 11 p.m. to 7:30 a.m. My tasks included check-in, check-out, welcoming the guests, serving drinks at the bar, running the vacuum cleaner and setting the tables for breakfast. I would finish the work in three hours and sit down to read or watch TV in the restaurant. Most nights the hotel was quiet, and there weren't many check-ins. I loved to work weekends because there were very few guests then, which meant there weren't many tables to set, and hardly anybody went in or out. Plus there was the Sunday erotic movie on TV. I hated it when there were large groups of guests at the hotel – tourists, sports people, business people, wedding guests and such. They would keep me working all night. They sat at the bar, schmoozing and ordering drink after drink, sometimes until dawn. I would go home in the morning and sleep until dusk.

Louise often came over in the evening, bringing food from her parents' house – pies, fruit, cooked vegetables. She introduced me to baby radish and avocado, both of which I immediately loved. On my off days, she would take me for a ride in the countryside in her vintage *deux chevaux*, two-horse-power Citroen. She was wonderful behind the wheel, smooth and confident. We went for walks in the countryside around Angers, napped under trees, made out in the car. We also went to the municipal swimming pool, where she tried to teach me to swim. I appreciated my girlfriend more every day. Sometimes she fell asleep by my side on the little bed, and I watched her sleep. It was a beautiful summer. Lazy, hazy and not so crazy.

Come September, they extended my contract at the hotel indefinitely. Laureline called. They were back in Angers after the roses in Belgium. Louise and I went to see them and found out that Laureline had left Tony and got together with Nick. I felt bad for Tony.

'It's karma. This is how it had to be,' said Laureline in-between puffs from a joint. She reminded me of Janis Joplin at that moment. Had Nick not been the beautiful person he was, I would have resented him for stealing Tony's girlfriend. Tony didn't come back to Angers. A few weeks later, Nick and Laureline left for England to pursue other plans. Louise took over their tiny apartment.

I enrolled for the second year of the English course at the university a third time, paid the fees, got proof of admission and went to file my visa application. At the visa office, I found myself face to face with one of the two unkind visa women I had had the displeasure of dealing with before. She took one look at my file and said, 'Monsieur, you can't submit a request for visa.'

'What do you mean? Why?' I said in dismay.

'You've stayed in the same class for the past two years without making any progress. This shows that you're incompetent to pursue studies in France. We deny your visa request and I invite you to leave French soil.'

My heart sank. I said I had been accepted by the university. She said it didn't matter and that I should have consulted the visa office first.

'*Mais Madame*, I didn't know, I didn't know,' I said desperately. I asked if there was a way out. She said it was possible to extend the visa if I enrolled in a different programme at the university, or in the same programme at a different uni but at a higher level. I left in a panic. God, what am I going to do? I wondered. It's too late to enrol in another programme. I can't go back to India. I can't return to that life of boredom and no jazz. I can't go back! I can't go back!

I called Louise and told her I was in deep shit. We met up at uni and I said I was fucked, I had no hope, I didn't know what to do, and I couldn't go back to India. I was horrified, my worst nightmare was coming true. Louise calmed me down a little and said we'd find a solution. My visa was valid until January 2003. In the next couple of days, I tried to look for another programme to enrol in. There was a possibility in a programme at the economics faculty. And I did enrol. But that was only a temporary solution. I couldn't come up with a new excuse every year, I had to end this visa problem for once and for all. Besides, as a student, I couldn't work full time nor could I search for jobs elsewhere in Europe.

'If I have to go back to India, I'll kill myself,' I told Louise. The idea of dying and going to hell was less horrifying than the thought of going back to India.

For the next few weeks, Louise and I had long discussions and debates on how to solve the problem. Finally we came to the inevitable conclusion that getting married was the only permanent solution. Neither of us wanted to get married nor were we ready to, she even less than I. But she wanted to do it for me, and I owe her eternal gratitude for that. We started to collect all the papers: birth certificates, police certificates, medical tests, my single status certificate from the Indian embassy in Paris. We weren't sure how long it was going to take to get all the required paperwork together, but at the city hall, we fixed a wedding date in December. At the same time, we couldn't help feeling anguished. Louise, naturally, was more worried than I was. For me, it was the solution to all my troubles, but she had to be careful about what kind of deal she was getting out of the compromise. In my most honest thoughts, I felt guilty about using her to save myself, but I had no choice. I promised myself I would be good to her.

The period before the wedding was fraught with doubts, anxieties, tearful arguments and even thoughts of calling it off. After one of our tiffs I said to myself that if she called off the wedding, I'd go back to India, learn Kalaripayyat in the south and come back to France as an instructor.

In early November, Louise had an ear operation. When I went to see her, with a rose and a Norman Rockwell calendar, she was under medication and acted tipsy. She took me in her arms and said in the cutest way, 'You want to marry me?'

Fifteen days before the wedding, we had a quiet quarrel. To cut a long story short, it was due to my selfish attitude and my constant preoccupation with myself. Now that I knew my problem was going to be solved, I had started taking Louise for granted. She came to my place meaning to talk about something and I kept reading a book, only half paying attention. She left, and later that evening, sent me a text message that said: 'You and I can't be together.' My heart sank, and my thoughts went to Kalaripayyat. The next morning, I called her and we went for a drive to the countryside.

She said I was too self-centred and didn't respect her enough. She wanted me to be interested in what she had to say and not be constantly absorbed in thoughts of myself, my life and my work. She wanted me to be more generous with time, attention and sympathy. I understood and promised to make an effort. I don't think she was totally convinced but she agreed to go ahead with the wedding. To be on the safe side, we went for a pre-nup, so that in case I had financial problems, she would not be held liable.

The preparations progressed without any interference on the part of Louise's parents. I had met them before, and they liked me. When Louise first spoke to her parents about getting married, they didn't freak out or anything, but told her to think about it seriously and do what she thought was right. Her grandparents, however, were not informed of our plans. Louise said they would certainly object, with their old-world views. She surmised they would say something like, 'If you get married to this guy he'll take you back to India and make you a slave.'

Not telling her grandparents was a big sacrifice on Louise's part, because they doted on her and would have loved to attend their only grandchild's wedding. But this was certain, had they been informed, it would never have gone as smoothly as it did. It still amazes me how totally independent Louise was in making such a big decision for herself. My stars were aligned just right. That's kismet. Being with the right person, in the right place, at the right time. I didn't feel the need to tell anyone in my family.

The night before our wedding, Louise and I went to bed together, without any apprehensions, looking forward to the morning. Our heads and hearts were clear of every doubt. I knew I was doing the right thing, and that I was going to be happy as a married man. I was going to love my wife for the kind and understanding person she was and for making such a huge sacrifice to save my ass.

The whole affair took five minutes. Louise drove us to the city hall in everyday clothes, the deputy mayor read us the vows, we signed, kissed and were off in no time. My witness was Rémi. Louise's witnesses were her best friends, Nico and Nellie. Nobody else was invited.

'Fuck, we're married!' I exclaimed as we stepped out of the townhall. Back at Louise's tiny studio, her other friends were waiting with some wonderful food. Louise's mother had brought over a delicious tagine and left before we arrived. The sobriety of the event was in keeping with my wish that there be no fanfare of any sort and no parents involved. Louise's parents respected that.

Voila, I was a married man at the age of twenty-five. It felt unreal, weird even. I felt I was too young to be married, and for a long time I had difficulty asserting my marital status before other people. My parents didn't know until Samar informed them six months later.

We celebrated Christmas that year at Louise's parents' place, and for New Year's Eve, we went to Louise's grandparents' house in Loches. We didn't want to tell them about the wedding yet.

Loches is a quaint medieval town with cobbled streets, creamy tuffeau stone buildings, triangular rooftops covered in grey slate, church spires, myriad weathercocks, smoke coming out of rectangular brick chimneys and stone walls going around the city. In the middle of all this rises the famous dungeon. Straight out of *Game of Thrones*.

The route to Loches traverses the beautiful countryside of the Loire Valley. It is flanked by trees, medieval churches, charming villages, troglodytes, vast hectares of private property with majestic manors lurking behind trees. Every few kilometres there is a sign signalling the presence of a historic monument – chateaux, abbeys, manors, windmills. The French cherish their monuments. The Indians piss and shit in theirs, and the Indian countryside looks good only in movies.

I thanked the Lord in my heart. I was where I wanted to be and it looked like it was going to be that way for a long time.

2003

13

We started looking for an apartment to move into together. I got busy with the Black History Month event that I had been planning with the American library. I wanted to perform Langston Hughes' poetry with jazz musicians, like Hughes himself on the *Weary Blues* record. When I suggested this to Yves, he agreed at once and got together a trio with his regular partners, drummer Franck and bassist Stéphane. I was on the fast lane to cultural emancipation, considering that three years ago I lived in India and knew very little about jazz. Not only that, I had no understanding of the basic concepts of music, like rhythm, notes and scales. Yet there I was, about to perform with professional jazz musicians!

I did feel a little uneasy about the idea of performing poetry by the poet laureate of Harlem on the occasion of Black History Month, when I was neither American nor black. But I had to do it. I really wanted to, and hey, nobody else seemed to have any qualms about my colour and nationality.

We rehearsed two or three times. The musicians were very inconsistent from one rehearsal to the next; they'd forget what we did the last time or how we had decided to perform a certain poem. Yves was always running off on other business before we had spent enough time rehearsing. It was chaotic, and I wondered what we would do on D day.

Seeing the event as an opportunity to mark my professional debut, I had convinced the library to pay us 150 euros each for the performance. The library, though normally lacking in funds, got some funding and gave me the money, and when I paid the musicians, I felt like a band leader in a jazz film.

The performance went well, though I was nervous and took frequent sips from my water bottle. But everyone seemed to enjoy it. The president of the library complimented me effusively. When I listened to the recording of the performance later, I was embarrassed about my accent and intonation. But looking back now, I think it wasn't too bad for a first-time, almost unrehearsed gig by a dude who had never done anything like that before. I would never have got that opportunity in India.

At the end of February, Louise went to Paris to prepare for an exam to become a dance instructor. Both of us have our respective areas of cultural expertise and action. Mine is jazz, hers is philosophy and contemporary dance. It's the kind of dance where dancers stand around making faces, twisting their limbs into distasteful positions, throwing around their bodies, falling to the ground, flashing boobs or jumping around shouting in foreign languages – a kind of abstract high art. Seriously though, while I'm caricaturing here, there is a lot of that stuff in contemporary dance. It's not really my thing, but the performances open up the mind and let you see how far people can go in the expression of their art. That in turn makes you bolder in your art. And in life.

Louise prepared for two months in Paris and went to Bordeaux to take the exam. She didn't clear it. I continued working at the hotel and we still had our own lodgings, though I was at Louise's place most of the time.

Shortly after the Black History Month event, I came across Joe McPhee's *Underground Railroad* record at the municipal library. I had never heard of him before but the cover art and the mention of Langston Hughes in the liner notes made me curious. 'Fuckin A!' I dug it from the very first minute. It was music that oozed unfettered freedom: the freedom to sing, dance, shout and scream through the music. That music did not mean to be a pretty crowd-pleaser, it meant to express itself. It had balls. It was raw and honest. Exactly the kind of art I craved. Exactly the kind of person I wanted to be.

That spurred me to give another listen to Anthony Braxton's '12 Alto Solos' which had been too dry for me a year ago. I loved it this time. The dry sound of the solo sax seeped into my soul like good red wine. And I was hooked. I listened to all the free jazz records available in the public library, read up all I could find on it and pretty soon felt like a connoisseur. The 'free' signifies freedom from the conventions and structures laid out by earlier forms of jazz. Free jazz opened up to me a whole new world of surprising new sounds – entire albums of saxophone solos, bass solos, trios with two basses, duos with trombone and voice and what not. And I began to rave about it with everybody I knew, like I do about all the new things I discover. On an impulse, I approached the local radio of Angers and proposed to do a free jazz show. They called me in for an audition and agreed to the show.

And that's how the *Free Jazz Experience* began. Every Thursday, 9 p.m. to 10 p.m., loads of great music by Albert Ayler, Archie Shepp and Roland Kirk floated on the airwaves in and around Angers. All borrowed from the library, where they had a great collection. The night I aired Muhal Richard Abrams' *Blues Forever* record, Rémi called and asked if I really enjoyed those esoteric, inaccessible sounds or whether I just wanted to feel like I was better than everybody else.

That summer, Louise and I found an apartment to our liking and budget, near Place Lafayette. Then Louise left to work at a summer camp for differently abled people. I wondered how she managed to drive around a bunch of people with mental deficiencies. Meanwhile, I moved house with the help of Louise's parents. They bought us a second-hand fridge and her father drilled holes in the walls to hang things. When Louise came back she painted the living room white with her grandfather's help. I outright refused to get my hands dirty. As a teenager I found the Asian Paints TV commercial where a couple paints their house so romantic. But there's really nothing romantic about sanding, cleaning and painting walls. I find it excruciatingly boring and time-consuming. In India, if you need something done, you call a guy to do it and you pay him. But here, labour costs are so high you're better off doing it yourself. DIY is a huge industry in France.

I bought a computer. That was a big deal for me because I had never owned a computer before and if I still lived in India, I'd never have the money to buy one. Over the next year, Rémi and Don came down to my place several times to get me out of some serious computer trouble.

The move gave me a sense of settling down. My fears and worries began to settle as well. And lust began to raise its head again. There's something about the summer here. It makes you horny.

Summers in India were a time of unbearable heat and sweat and dust and hot winds and long powercuts. In school, I would wonder why, in songs and poems from Europe and America, summer was such a splendid period associated with easy living and carefree loving. Now I know. Summer is, in fact, a glorious time in this part of the world. School is over, flowers are blooming, birds are chirping, bees are mating. And it makes you very horny, maybe because you see more female skin or have more time or some such thing. I began to ask myself if I would be able to carry on with my life without touching another woman. I was like Tomas from *The Unbearable Lightness of Being*. I was curious about women and desirous of discovering the unique thrills that each one had in store. I mean, what was the point of living in this land of beauty and sex if I didn't enjoy it as much as I could? I knew it wouldn't be right to Louise but I didn't want to live a repressed life. Pent-up sexual desires are known to drive you nuts. All psychos have a history of sexual repression. I would have to give into my lust for the sake of my sanity. What would you do if your sanity was at stake? Everybody who gets a chance to do it, does it. Tigers do it, Clintons do it, even Kennedys do it. Besides, fidelity is a manmade concept, contrary to our animal nature. I wish we were all hippies and lived in a carefree world of peace and free love where we would all be sexually fulfilled and devote our energies to higher pursuits. Also, logically, if the Lord put other women in my path, it was the Lord's will. So I decided to let my natural instincts take the lead.

The Lord's will manifested itself pretty quickly. At the hotel, I had a passing tryst with the new receptionist who worked the evening shift until 11 p.m., after which I took over for the night. Our paths crossed often. One night, I was watching TV in the dining hall when she reappeared at the door – she said she had forgotten her keys. The hotel was quiet, the bar deserted. I asked her to stay and have a drink, she settled for coffee. We talked. She had recently come back to France after spending two years in Italy with her boyfriend. They had split up now. She asked me if I had a girlfriend. I said no. She said that after work that evening she had gone to a bar with some friends where something had happened to stress her out. She finished her coffee and began to rise.

'Are you still feeling stressed?'

'Yes,' she said.

'I can help. Sit down and give me your hand.' She obeyed. I took her left hand and started massaging it. Then her right hand. Then both arms, placing my hand on her upper arm and sliding it down to the fingertips in a gentle caress. I stood behind the couch to work on her shoulders. She seemed to enjoy it. I proceeded to work on her neck. From behind the couch, I reached down across her full bosom, undid the top button of her jacket and rolled back the collars to make room for my hands on her neck. She closed her eyes, leaned back and relaxed. I caressed the skin under her shoulder-length hair. 'That feels nice,' she murmured.

I reached around her then and kissed her lips. Her eyes opened. She responded for about two seconds and then stopped. I straightened myself and resumed the massage. She just sat there. I tried to kiss her again but she began to get up. I held her back by the shoulders and concentrated on the massage. Then I came in front and placed my hands on her calves to massage her legs.

'No, not the legs, I'm very ticklish there,' she said with a start. I tried to kiss her again but she held back. Finally she rose to go, saying that with my skills as a masseur, it was hard to believe that I didn't have a girlfriend. She wasn't being sarcastic, she was genuinely impressed. Nevertheless, she left without giving me the tongue-tangler I was looking forward to. She wasn't that into me, I guess. I should have accompanied the massage with some sex talk, like Tony.

Nothing happened between us again and she quit the job soon after.

Then there was this waitress who worked the breakfast shift. She was nice, she liked me, even teased me now and then. She was a typical country gal with a Breton name, a freckled face and average looks, meant for small-time work. But her ass was full and juicy. I wanted to grab it. In fact, I got a little obsessed with it. One morning, as she was operating the dishwasher, I went into the kitchen and placed my hand on her ass.

'You threw the spoon in the waste bin,' she said, shifting her ass away from under my hand. I just looked at her, in a trance. 'You threw the spoon in the waste bin,' she repeated and the trance broke. I had indeed thrown a spoon in the waste bin. Then I left the kitchen. I didn't try anything with her again. I learnt later that she was married and had a kid. She remained friendly. That's the great thing about living in France. If you're an agreeable person, your occasional indiscretions and sexual transgressions are quickly forgotten, or at least set aside. Women don't think of you as a monster for trying to get physical with them as long as it's done in a gentle manner. I think they even find it flattering.

I discovered prepaid telephone cards that made calling India much cheaper and started calling my parents more regularly. With dad, the conversation was just 'Hi, hello, how are you?' He had retired last year and now lived on the first floor of his brother's house in Mohali. Mom still lived in the one-room house in Masti. She had nowhere else to go. She would tell me stories about our relatives and whatever was happening in India – Dev Anand receiving an honour, Amitabh Bachchan's illness, the food adulteration scam, the counterfeit currency frauds and so on. I told mom I was worried about the future and felt guilty about not being able to send her enough money. She told me not to worry about anything and to just keep looking for ways to improve my life, and warned me never to give up. She said you get what you get in life when the time is right. She said it was a good thing I didn't live in India, for I wasn't meant to live there, and if I did I would go crazy. My thoughts exactly.

One summer evening, at Louise's parents' place, there was a story on TV about illegal immigration in France. It showed a couple of illegal immigrants from India being put on a plane. They were strait-jacketed and kept shouting, 'Nahin jayenge! Nahin jayenge!' My heart went out to them and a chill went down my spine as I imagined myself in that situation. I tried to imagine where I would be if I lived in India, and shuddered. I would most certainly end up in a mad-house. I still had the occasional nightmare about having to go back to India. The kind of nightmare that makes you moan in helpless agony and wake up in sweat.

Louise had planned a surprise for our first wedding anniversary – a weekend trip to Venice. We took the night train from Paris. As soon as we arrived in Venice, Louise wanted us to buy a 72-hour pass for the vaporetto, the waterbus that takes you across the canals. It was expensive, so I wanted to wait until the next day to see if we really needed the passes. We got into a fight over it of course. To her, I was the killjoy who always said no to spending money. Finally I let her buy the passes just to shut her up. We took the vaporetto to the other side of the canal and went to the hotel. Louise had the map and insisted on leading the way. But she got it all wrong. When I tried to reason with her, she began to shout at me. I lost my temper and we had a bad argument. I told her to go fuck herself. I don't recall all the mean things we said to each other, but it was ugly. She sat down on the steps of one of those myriad little Venetian bridges and sobbed for twenty minutes before I consoled her and took us to the hotel.

Our room was charming, it altered our mood and we became friends again. After some rest, we roamed the streets of Venice, checking out everything on the way. The next day, we were informed that the vaporettos were on a weekend strike. And I wished my hard-headed wife had listened to me and not bought the tickets. The strike also prevented us from going to the island of Murano to see the blown-glass industry.

We walked through Venice, eating delicious pizza and drinking hot chocolate. It was real hot chocolate, unlike the piss-warm milk and powder served in French cafés. I had the best ever margherita pizza at a small hole-in-the wall pizzeria. It was simple, thin and soft and served as a roll. Venice is a tiny, beautiful and expensive city with canals, narrow streets, little bridges and open markets. Loads of tourists. And you hear French everywhere. Apparently, the population and prices triple during the carnival period. We visited the wonderful mask shop that had supplied masks for *Eyes Wide Shut* and I found some rare CDs at very cheap prices.

Louise and I had another fight on the day of our departure, then another one on our arrival in Paris. But we got back home in one piece. We spent Christmas in Loches again, and this time we informed Louise's grandparents of the wedding. They took it rather well – they were perhaps more used to me by now.

2004

14

On the first of January, we woke up to a glorious snowfall, my first ever. We were at Louise's grandparents' house, and the four of us spent all morning in the snow, having snow fights and building a snowman in the middle of the garden. At her grandmother's suggestion, we adorned it with a carrot for a cock. When we returned to Angers, we threw a soirée for friends at our apartment.

Louise and I were still learning to live together. We decided I would do the dishes and the vacuum cleaning, and she would cook. I loved her cooking and she baked the most sublime cakes. She also had a talent for making food out of practically nothing. From time to time, I'd cook dal-chawal with onions, ginger, garlic, tomatoes and curry powder. She loved to see me cook. She thought a man in the kitchen was a sexy sight.

With the good came the bad. We fought a lot. It was a new experience for both of us. Not just the newness of living with someone but living with someone who was so different. Different temperaments, different outlooks to life, different levels of patience, different ambitions. Well, I had no patience and she had no ambition. She was gentle, attentive and generous, while I was self-centred and stingy with money and time. She wanted my attention and I wanted to attend to my goals, namely, a job and money, and was constantly worried about getting somewhere in life. She wanted to go to the cinema and I wanted to sit at my computer. She wanted to eat out but I didn't want to spend money. She wanted to go for a walk in the countryside while I wanted to stay in and read.

I don't know when I became this way, a nay-sayer with a constant frown. Before we were married, I said yes to most things. Post-wedding, I said more no than yes. I think my mindset was, okay, now that I can stay in France I've got to do something worthwhile with my life. And I worried about it all the time. The more I worried, the more I retreated into my shell and the more negative I became. And this inner turmoil caused us to fight. A lot.

At first they were just verbal arguments. But gradually, we started to inflict light physical violence upon each other. I started it, but she forced me to. When she was unhappy about something she'd go on and on about it, berating me in a voice that made me lose patience. I had never thought I would hit my wife, and I had always told myself that I would never fight like my parents did, but in the end I was no different from my dad. I could see him in me, and there were moments when I thought I actually was him: the way I scrunched my face in frustration, when I broke a glass in anger or when I threw a book at Louise in an erratic burst of rage. I was becoming him. I made her cry and she wept like I had never seen anyone weep. I felt like an evil cunt, mean and ungrateful. After a fight she would close the bedroom door and go to sleep. But I was always watchful, fearing she would creep up on me from behind and hit me with something. Like my mom did to my dad. I was getting paranoid. Sometimes I wondered what I had got myself into.

Eventually, in my quest for marital harmony and peace, I noticed a pattern. Louise was more irritable and unpleasant around her period and we had a massive fight every two months. I took these observations into consideration and made adjustments to my general attitude. I tried to be more attentive, less selfish and more positive. It takes a lot of effort to change the way you've thought and lived all your life. I tried to meditate regularly to help me in my endeavour.

When we were not fighting, we were busy with our respective lives or having a nice meal together or laughing about my *faux pas* in French. I had so much to learn from Louise about the language, culture and food of France. We talked about our differences in thinking and personality. She said she had never known anyone with my attitude, outlook and general disposition – and she didn't always mean this as a compliment – and in her opinion, we were so different that if we were not married we wouldn't even be friends. I agreed. She said she had never in her wildest dreams imagined getting married to a hairy Indian, but she liked being my wife. As for me, I had never thought I would be married to a French girl, I mean, I hadn't even thought I'd get out of India. And here we were, living as Monsieur and Madame Singh.

It's strange when you think about it, how people's lives change. When I was still in school, my mother used to say that she'd find me a girl who could sing. Well, I'd found that girl myself. Louise sang beautifully and even invented funny song lyrics when she was in the mood.

Curious cat that she was, she bought a French–Hindi dictionary. I hadn't even known such a thing existed. She also read up on the history of the Sikhs. I taught her a bit of Hindi too. She wrote the word 'titli', butterfly, on a slate and we hung it in the kitchen. When I called mom, Louise would speak to her in a bit of broken Hindi and English – 'Hello, Sat sri akal. Kya haal hai?'

Every two or three months we went to spend the weekend with Louise's grandparents. Her grandmother would welcome us with a lunch of roast chicken and potatoes with red wine. We would laze about in the big garden or go for a stroll in the city or to the surrounding countryside, where I checked out the old houses and churches. I loved those small village churches. Even the tiniest village in France had at least one ancient church. The churches had this old-world atmosphere with sculptures and high ceilings, and chants emanating from discreetly placed cylindrical Bose speakers. I wanted to sit down on the centuries-old benches and soak in the vibes for hours, but we never had the time. I fantasized about having free jazz orgies in one of those churches.

15

I had begun to think of Angers as my native city, and in a way it was. I had started a new life here and discovered my *joie de vivre*. I loved the architecture, clean tuffeau stone buildings, beautiful women and distinctive bourgeois charm. It was not too big, not too small and always full of sunshine. The city was overflowing with lovely young women, thanks to the two universities and several graduate schools. A new crop arrived every year. And it was chic, thanks to the high bourgeois population.

I think it was this year that I began to distinguish between the bourgeois and the non-bourgeois. There is a marked class distinction in France, based on what family you come from, what you have studied, where you go on vacation, the way you carry yourself, the way you talk, etc. The bourgeois ladies have distinguishable traits: they wear the chicest brands in the latest trends, look elegant in their pricey trench coats with collars yanked up and pearls around the neck, they hold themselves erect and walk fast listening to their iPods or talking on their iPhones. They have girlfriends who dress like they do and they all wear their coiffured hair in similar fashion, with one side of the forehead hidden under forelocks. It seems to be the signature of their clique. Their boyfriends are equally chic and branded, with yanked up collars on Lacoste t-shirts. These birds live in the same part of the city, the bourgeois sector. They all go to the expensive Catholic University or to business school and their parents are lawyers, doctors, dentists, vets, public notaries, top executives, landlords... you get the picture. They also tend to lean to the political right. Maybe that's the reason why the bourgeois babes didn't give a fuck about my exoticism. Their upbringing conditions them to be attracted only to their kind. They won't even look at you if you don't belong where they belong. Unless, of course, you look like Brad Pitt.

As homage to Angers, my film-maker friend Roger and I started to make a short street-movie. The only character in the movie was me, wandering around the city and walking past its landmarks to a free jazz soundtrack. We shot bits and parts over the next year but never finished it. In the footage, there's a great candid scene with me bopping the boner to the sounds of Albert Ayler's 'The Truth Is Marching In'. Meanwhile, the *Free Jazz Experience* continued. The DJ who occupied the slot just before mine broadcasted songs from the Antilles with vulgar lyrics. He said he liked my show and suggested I write to record labels and ask for promotional CDs. I took his advice and wrote to a few independent labels, and hallelujah, in a few weeks I got my first fat packet of CDs – a host of unfamiliar names playing enthralling music. Until now, I had been listening to and airing mainly the classic '60s and '70s American free jazz, but this was the free jazz of today, by both American and European musicians. More new music arrived and the show began to thrive. I wondered what Kerouac would say about free jazz. Going by his love of freedom and spontaneity, I believe he would dig it.

That February, I got a few hours of teaching work at the Cosmodemonic Language School which had recently opened at Place de la Visitation, a five-minute walk from my place. Life dragged on uneventfully, working at the hotel, teaching English, promoting free jazz through radio and gigs, worrying about my parents, trying to figure out the purpose of my life. The biggest problem in my life has always been determining what I want. If you know what you want, half your life is already sorted. If you know the destination you will certainly find a way to get there. I knew I didn't want to be a loser all my life but I had no idea what I had to be to not be a loser. This year, I decided I wanted to work with jazz musicians. I helped Yves with his Ornette Coleman tribute project, made brochures and sent them to festival directors. I also looked for jobs at jazz festivals and clubs. No luck.

In March, I applied for a training programme in music production at a school that specialized in the music industry. This qualification would allow me to work with tour operators and music festivals. I also applied for a CIF grant. CIF is a thing in the French employee system where the state gives an employee substantial financial help to pursue studies in any field with the objective of changing careers. It's a one-time opportunity. I made a solid dossier and wrote a convincing letter of motivation with Louise's help and was granted a CIF for the entire duration of my programme. They would pay me my current monthly salary and a monthly travel allowance. I couldn't have asked for more. Vive la France!

Then came the admission interview at the school, and they rejected me. I felt awful about it then, but later figured it was a good thing, because that wasn't what I really wanted to do. My CIF money remained untouched and I could use it at a later time, for something better.

In April, Manmohan Singh became the first Sikh prime minister of India, and the Sikh community around the world chanted 'Singh is king'. I joined driving school. Where an average person needs about thirty hours of instruction and one to three tries to pass the test, over the next year and a half, I took over seventy hours of driving lessons and failed the test twice. I didn't have the time or the money to try a third time. In India, you'd learn to drive with your daddy's car and then buy a driving licence. My daddy only had a scooter.

In June, we went to Denmark for Hemming's wedding. He and his girlfriend had got back together and decided never to part again. We arrived a few days before the wedding and participated in the preparations. The wedding took place in a little church in Nykobing Falster. It was a quick ceremony, followed by a reception with tea, coffee, cake, whiskey, cognac, Baileys and Gammel Dansk. While getting myself a drink, I exchanged a few words with a really beautiful girl, Camilla. She looked a bit jittery. I wanted to get to know her. As luck would have it, at the dinner table, Louise and I were seated facing Camilla and her boyfriend. We made further acquaintance. Everybody was given disposable cameras to take pictures at will. Family and friends made speeches in Danish. I made an impromptu speech in English about how Hemming and I first met. Pontus interpreted it in Danish. At my request, Hemming picked up his guitar and did 'Blue Suede Shoes', singing and dancing just like the old days. It was awesome. More than once, I caught Camilla staring at me and began to feel jittery myself. Concupiscentia carnis was kicking in.

After dinner, it was time to dance. A salsa band from Copenhagen was playing. I danced with Louise a little, then sat while she danced with Jens. After a while I went over to where the guests had put their presents. Camilla was there. We remarked on the presents, she said something about the band and dancing. I said I didn't like dancing much because I didn't have a sense of rhythm. She said, 'Shall we try? Let's go dance.' How could I refuse? Louise was dancing with someone else now. I was very self-conscious, not just about the dancing but also about the surge of desire I was feeling for the Danish doll. She was gorgeous, with wide Nordic lips, brown eyes, long, curly, brown-blond hair and a gorgeous body. I couldn't help tell her that she was beautiful. She blushed and said thank you. Then we drifted away. I wanted to kiss her so much. I knew she felt something for me but it was hard to determine to what degree. The music and dancing continued till the wee hours of the morning before we all went to bed. I thought about Camilla and imagined all kinds of situations where I would kiss and caress her curves. In the morning, everybody left. I kept thinking of Camilla.

In Copenhagen, Louise and I had a huge quarrel over something. It was my fault, I was unpleasant with her, and it was because my head was full of Camilla. I'll spare you the details. Louise was so pissed off she wanted to take the plane back to Paris that very day.

In September, Cosmodemonic employed me full time. Let me bring you up to speed on this shitty business. It's a chain of English language training schools, based on principles very similar to McDonald's. And like McDonald's, it has spread its tentacles all over Europe. The franchise in Angers is owned by an asshole called Samuel Troudecul. Shortly after Troudecul gave me a full-time contract, the service manager, Rich Adams, a nice British guy, was demoted to the position of teacher and Carine Saloppe became the manager. Carine the cunt was this rather good-looking but spiteful little bitch who was a teacher at Cosmodemonic and always had her eye on Rich's job. She was certain she could do the job better, which wasn't entirely untrue. She and the account executive, Vincent Connard, had started sleeping together sometime in the beginning of the year, They both hated Troudecul. Actually, everybody hated Troudecul.

To give the devil his due, Connard was real good at selling. He was the guy who brought in the clients and made Troudecul all the money he was stuffing into his pocket. Connard must have sold his mother to the devil right after he was born. Rich's downfall was obviously the handiwork of the Connard-Saloppe team. Then there were the stupid clients to deal with. Teaching English to the French can be a nightmare. They keep asking 'why?', they want rules and reasons for everything, as if learning English were a scientific experiment. The upside of the job was that I came in contact with the young female trainees floating in and out of the place, and fantasized about some of them. So much so that on more than one occasion, I had to head to the toilet to make peace with the capricious little bastard that lives in my underwear. You ever get to do that at work?

In November, Anthony Braxton came to the cultural centre of La Roche-sur-Yon with his new quartet. I called the cultural centre and they arranged for me to interview Mr Braxton. We spoke about his music, American politics, Langston Hughes, Jack Kerouac, Elvis Presley. He said nobody had ever asked him about Elvis or Kerouac. It was a big day for me, the realization of a dream.

In December, Samar and dad visited Angers. Samar had flown to India from Australia, picked up dad and brought him to France. It had been five years since I had seen them. Samar, five foot eight and clean-shaven, had been living in Sydney since 2001 and had started working at National Australia Bank this year. He was doing well for himself. He always had been a bright, hardworking go-getter. We had kept in touch all these years, through telephone and email, talking about our jobs, lives and what we could do to help our parents financially.

The fact that I had been unkind to my brother when we were kids had weighed on my conscience for a long time. I had nightmares where I saw myself beating him up. Those dreams always made me feel guilty and left me feeling disturbed. I used to beat him up bad, like a fucking animal. There was this one time I remembered so vividly that every time I thought about it, it felt like a scene from a movie I had recently watched. It filled me with such profound guilt that I felt like crying. And I did cry, a couple of times. It happened when we lived in Masti. I had an old tape recorder and I needed to record a speech that I was practising for school.

I asked Samar to push the record button when I was ready. I told him to make sure he was recording side B of the cassette because on side A there were some Dev Anand songs. When I finished, I realized that the speech had been recorded on the wrong side. I was furious and hit Samar, he tried to get away but I caught him by the arm, grabbed a thick painting brush and started poking it into his belly mercilessly. And that wasn't the only time. I tortured him in many different ways on many different occasions. Why was I so mean? Was it the frustration of not having a normal family?

All that changed with age and I became quite protective of my brother when we went to Five Rivers. Thankfully, he stayed in that hellhole of a boarding school for just two months, after which dad took him back to our old school in Masti. Then he went to St Lawrence in Dehradun. My brother spoke highly of me at his new school. I heard from his teachers that he said, 'My brother is a genius.' He must have meant something like 'My brother is a great guy' or 'I love my brother.' Because I was pretty average at everything I did.

I guess he doesn't think of me the same way today. I'm an obvious failure and have wasted precious time not doing anything worthwhile. There's one thing, though, I did contribute to Samar's culture in some ways. Thanks to me, he got to listen to classic Hindi film songs and rock 'n' roll. And I don't think he would have read books like *The Fountainhead* and *The Godfather* if it hadn't been for me.

Samar brought me a saxophone made in India, which turned out to be a piece of junk, unplayable, and a specimen of tawdry craftsmanship. Ten thousand rupees down the drain. He also brought my copy of *Madhushala*. I had forgotten to pack it with my stuff in 2000. I had added a verse of my own to the poem when I was nineteen. My verse ends with '*Jeevan ka mridu pee mein mast/ mujh mein hee hai madhushala.*' I am drunk on the nectar of life/ the madhushala resides inside me.

Both dad and Samar loved Louise. And dad loved the fact that the French were such courteous people.

'People are so nice here. Always smiling. You bump into someone accidentally and they smile and say sorry. In India they say, "What the hell, you blind or what?"' dad remarked. We went for drives, walks and drinks. One night, we walked from our place to the narrow cobbled streets of La Doutre across the river, Samar, Louise and I. Samar and I had a semi-serious conversation about career and money.

'So, what do you want to do with your life? You've got to do something more worthwhile.'

'Yes, I should. But I don't know what to do,' I said.

'You've got to make more dough, bro. We both need to make dough if we want to take care of our parents,' he said.

'I agree but I have no ideas. I don't know which way to go. I worry about it all the time.'

'You should read *Rich Dad, Poor Dad* by Robert Kiyosaki. Maybe you'll learn something.'

Samar and I talked about a lot of things but my communication with dad remained as awkward as it was on the phone. We didn't have much to say to each other. He would just sit in the living room ruminating. Louise made him talk when she asked him questions.

On Samar's birthday, he insisted we go to the disco. There was Louise's friend Audrey, Audrey's sister Nico, Louise, Samar and myself. We danced and drank. There were three very fuckable girls on the dance floor. I kept checking out their asses when Louise was not looking. A drunken floozy came on to me while I was ordering a drink at the bar.

'You got a cigarette?' she asked, coming very close, almost falling against me. I would have gladly offered her my cigar to blow if my wife weren't around. I said I didn't have a cigarette, and she went in another direction. It was a good evening, and it was the first and only time Samar and I were in a disco together. He totally lived up to his reputation.

We spent Christmas at Loches and New Year's Eve at our place in Angers. It wasn't the best New Year's Eve. There was Don, Amélie, Laurie and his crazy girlfriend who was high on something. Samar saw her steal cigarettes from Louise's bag. She also grabbed my camera and took some lousy pictures. The atmosphere wasn't great, we just sat there and talked like a bunch of people who had nothing to say to each other. My brother would have preferred to go out and party.

2005

16

In the first week of January, we took dad and Samar to Paris for a couple of days. Stayed at Nico's tiny apartment on the sixth floor of an old building. We walked along the Seine and visited all the landmarks: Les Champs Elysées, Monmartre, Quartier Latin, Moulin Rouge. We arrived at the Louvre in the nick of time and Samar bought a ticket and dashed off to see the Mona Lisa. At the Eiffel Tower, Samar climbed up to the top, leaving Louise and me with dad on the lawns. Then came the day of departure. Dad got all emotional at the train station and his eyes watered. Louise teared up too. I felt sad. Samar looked like he didn't care.

While the world was reeling with the devastation caused by the tsunami and debates about the environment were on the surge, I found a PDF of *Rich Dad, Poor Dad* for fifty cents on eBay and read the entire book in three weeks. Robert Kiyosaki's philosophy hit home: don't work for money, make money work for you.

In January, there was a new trainee at Cosmodemonic, Capucine Belfess. Her first class was with me. She did not exactly hit me between the eyes. She was a serious lady, barely smiled when I said hello. I thought she was okay-looking, with a full mouth, light lipstick and a head of light brown hair. She looked like she was in her thirties and she probably had kids. She had to prepare a job interview for a company in the US. She had brought a CV to work with. The CV said marital status: single.

'You're single. What a bummer, I'm married,' I joked. She looked at me without smiling. She didn't get what I said and I didn't bother explaining.

We sat across each other at the little round table. In the first hour, I discovered that her English was not bad at all. I put her at ease and made her smile a few times. As she relaxed, she looked more attractive. I suggested taking a break before starting the next hour. As I opened the door for her and she went out, I was dazzled by the sight of her derrière, big, round and tight. It totally got my tongue wagging in my pants. We had coffee, she laughed at all my jokes. She had small breasts, big teeth and a wide smile that made you want to take a bite of her luscious lips and slide your tongue between them. Beautiful blue eyes that made you want to dive into them, and into her.

Capucine was on an accelerated one-on-one course and had frequent classes with me. The more we saw each other, the more she relaxed. The more she relaxed, the better she looked. The better she looked, the more I wanted her.

She was a biologist working on a new formula for an anti-wrinkle cream. She already had a couple of patents to her name and was looking to present her research to a pharmaceutical firm in Boston. And so, we talked about molecules, proteins, enzymes and life in general. She said she liked to sketch. I asked to see her sketches and she brought them in the next time. I complimented her on her dress. I asked her things like 'What makes you happy in life? What do you want from life?' I asked that of all the pretty girls. I learnt that from *On The Road*. These are potent questions if you want to establish an emotional rapport with women, and I could feel the rapport with Capucine.

One Saturday afternoon, while I was in the staff room packing up to leave, I saw her come out of another class.

'Hey, you want to go for a drink?' I asked after a second of gathering my balls.

'Yes,' said Capucine.

We went to Bar du Centre in her car. She smoked and we talked. That day I knew for sure we had chemistry and that a synthesis could be envisaged.

On a Monday afternoon, some weeks later, she informed me that it was her last day at Cosmodemonic. She had done the number of hours her current employer had paid for. I said that was unfortunate, but we could carry on informal sessions outside Cosmodemonic.

'Yes, that would be nice, we could go for a drink and speak in English.' She sounded delighted.

'How about this Wednesday?'

'Okay.'

'Around 10 p.m.?'

'Why so late?' she said, wide-eyed.

'Well, I finish here at eight, then go home, eat and maybe take a shower before going out, you know.'

'Okay,' she nodded with a smile.

The real reason behind that late date was to get Louise's customary phone call out of the way. Louise had recently joined a course in dance education in Tours. She was there from Tuesday to Friday and called every night.

On Wednesday, after Louise's call, I waited for Capucine at Ralliement. She showed up, her hair pulled back tight. She looked like a mature business woman on a night out. We shook hands and went looking for a suitable bar. I led the way and apologized for not having had the time to decide on a place. 'There,' she said teasingly, pointing at a gay bar. 'Or there,' pointing at the cinema. We finally went to Sunset.

It had recently been redecorated. We sat in a corner on the mezzanine. She took off her coat, revealing a crisp white shirt, and loosened her hair.

'You are beautiful,' I said. I do not recall the superficial conversation we had before I expressed the desire to get out of there. She nodded in agreement. I led the way and we strolled through the old city towards the chateau. The old city is the perfect setting for a seduction walk. The narrow cobblestone streets are abandoned, with a streetlight here and there, and walking on the uneven surface allows for unintended brushing of the arms.

We stood at the edge of the old city by the castle – they call it *le bout du monde*, the end of the world – and looked at the cars on the highway. I felt an urge to grab her from behind but thought better of it. Then we strolled back through the cobblestone streets, across Ralliement, along Boulevard Foch, into Jardin du Mail. I have no idea what we spoke about, I was distracted by my cell phone vibrating in my pants. It was Louise calling, of course. She had a flair for making her presence felt exactly when I could do without it. I didn't answer.

Capucine suggested we sit down on a bench in the park. She gazed at the fountain in front of us while I sat on her left, my body half turned towards her, my right hand resting on the back of the bench. I looked at her and thought of telling her that I was a married man, but thought better of it. Instead, I decided to test the theory that women like it when men whisper in their ear. I leaned closer and said in a low voice, 'You know what, your molecular structure is something else.' She looked at me for two seconds, and then a toothy smile appeared.

'And your smile is a killer.' The smile broadened, almost a laugh. Our mouths were just six inches apart.

'I love your hair,' I whispered.

'Mmn hmm,' she said, only half looking at me, nodding and smiling.

'I'd like to sing you a song,' I said, tracing the outline of her face with my finger.

'Mmn hmm.'

'Would you like me to sing you a song?' She nodded. In my raunchiest Kishore Kumar voice, I hummed into her ear, '*Hum hain raahi pyar ke, hum se kuchh na boliye...*' I wanted to kiss her but wasn't sure. '*...dard bhi hume kabool...*' and my mouth touched her cheek close to her ear. She hesitated and then looked at me, an impish smile playing on her lips and glittering eyes that said, 'There we are.'

I gave her my most charming smile, looked into her eyes and said, 'I also love the taste of your skin,' and leaned forward to kiss her on the lips. She pulled back. I looked at her with questioning eyes.

'I'm not feeling very good,' she said.

'A kiss will make you feel good,' I said, my right hand already on her lower back. She smiled, shook back her hair, pressed her lips and looked at me as if she was deciding whether or not to be kissed. I took her hand in mine, looked into those blue eyes for fifteen seconds, trying to hypnotize her, and then I placed my lips on hers. She responded. The kiss progressed beautifully. My left hand reached for her waist inside her coat. Then we detached ourselves and looked at each other. Once again I suppressed the urge to tell her the truth. I was worried that somebody who knew Louise and me might walk in on us. Angers is such a small town. I volunteered to walk her home. We didn't say much on the way. I cooed into her ear inanities like 'You are something else!' and 'Your eyes are like the beautiful lakes of Kashmir.'

Capucine lived in an apartment building near the conservatory. She invited me upstairs for a cup of tea. Exactly what I'd been hoping for. I love tea. We entered the building and went up the stairs to the second floor. She fumbled for her keys, not looking at me, blushing, perhaps imagining what lay ahead. Her apartment was quite spacious, the furniture arranged prettily, tastefully large windows, a shelf with books and CDs, a fancy stereo. The bed looked comfortable and the rooms smelled clean. I took off my jacket and sat down on the couch. She proceeded to boil water for tea, her back turned to me. I was so aroused I wanted to reach out, grab that ass, shake off my jeans and go right in. But such eagerness might jeopardize the mission with a French woman. I stayed put. We talked while the water boiled. She told me she had broken up this morning with a man she was going out with. It was a difficult relationship because the guy was married. My heart was in my mouth when she said that. We sat down on the couch and sipped our tea, and my heart returned to its normal place.

'I have a great technique to help you feel better,' I said. She smiled knowingly.

'It's not what you think. I'll show you what I mean.' I stood up, made my way behind the couch and started caressing her hair, then dug deeper and started massaging her scalp and neck. The old routine, you know. 'You like it?' She said it was soothing. When she was sufficiently relaxed, I kissed her on the cheek, the neck… She sat there enjoying the experience. I nibbled at her ear and my left hand slipped down to her left breast. It was a snug fit in my palm. She let out a sigh that confirmed that I could advance without fear. I kissed and nibbled her ear some more while gently kneading her breasts over her shirt, then I walked around to the front of the couch and we kissed. I sat astride her thighs and my hands roamed all over her body. She sat there in a trance, just feeling the feeling. I unbuttoned her shirt and kissed her between the breasts, and proceeded to set them free from her lacy bra.

She finally came to life and tugged at my sweater. I took it off, along with my shirt. I kissed her breasts, and kneeled on the floor to kiss her stomach, I unbuttoned her jeans and ran my tongue along the off-white panties. Her milky smooth thighs were the stuff of my wettest dreams. I caressed her and kissed between her legs before she led me to her bed. I lay on her full-length, and let our bodies rub together, my chest mashing her breasts and my lower half grinding her glory. I kissed her along the side of her body and turned her over. The undulations of that body were to die for. Words can't describe the lust I felt at the sight of all that copious curvaceousness lying before me. I wanted to get inside all that golden flesh and romp around like crazy. I wanted to kiss it, lick it, bite it, chew it and beat my meat on it. Total pervy stuff.

I came as I was taking her from behind, kneading those hemispheres of desire, lost in the music of her moaning. I think I came too soon. I always come too soon. Well, better soon than never, I suppose.

Walking back home that night, I felt the tingling taste of the forbidden fruit turn into sour feelings of guilt.

On Friday, after some making out, I spilled the beans. I told her I was married. It was a shock to her and she refused to continue with the relationship. To tell you the truth, now that I had fulfilled my lust, the excitement was wearing off and the fear of being caught was taking over. I was too afraid to carry on and wanted to give her a reason to end it. I was afraid of Louise. If she got whiff of the affair – which she most certainly would, for Angers is a small town and I am an incompetent liar – she would hurt herself or me or us both. I wanted Capucine to kick me out before it was too late. And she did.

Post-Capucine, at Cosmodemonic, I gave a one-on-one class to this cute girl with sparkling eyes and a mouth-watering rearview. She totally lit my fire. I asked her, 'What makes you happy in life?' We had a nice conversation about her likes and dislikes. In the end, I said, 'All right then, have a good evening and a good dinner.'

'Yeah... alone,' she said wistfully. I made a sympathetic face, pressed my lips together and said like a preacher, 'Sometimes we're alone, at other times we're not.'

Now why would I do that? Well, because I knew my wife was waiting for me at home with dinner on the table and I had no excuse not to go home right after work. If Louise had not been home, my response to the girl would have been, 'Oh, really, I'm having dinner alone as well. Let's eat together.' Whether that would have led to us eating each other is a whole different matter. Point is, I'd do my karma. I think I subconsciously saw sexual conquest as a way of compensating for the material success I so longed for but didn't know how to achieve. I mean, it was a substitute as well as a vent to the frustration of not making it. It was like I can't make money but I can still make honey!

Sometime this year, I connected with a free jazz fan called Chaamba. He had discovered my radio show blog and emailed to say that he dug the music. We met in Paris and got along well. Then on, every time I went to Paris, I stayed at his place in République, until he moved to Brittany in 2007. In Paris, we would go out, eat tandoori chicken at an Indian restaurant and stroll about, feasting our eyes on Parisian women. That city, folks, is a fathomless sea of unbelievably attractive women, pouring in from all over the world. Arriving at the train station at Montparnasse, you're swept by waves of young, lusty female bosoms and the most stupefying asses going in every direction, climbing up and down the myriad staircases leading to the trains.

Chaamba was in his early forties and a most ordinary looking guy, of average height and a laid-back demeanour. But what do they say about book covers and judgement? Contrary to all appearances, Chaamba was a fucking sex machine. Women were attracted to him like bees to honey, flies to shit, kids to candy. When I met him, he was going out with a bourgeois woman about his age. Some months later – and this is incredible – he met a twenty-three-year-old *chica* from Chile on Soulseek! Let me explain why this is so amazing. Soulseek is a P2P portal for sharing free jazz and such music. The fans of this music are predominantly male and you'll never run into a girl who knows shit about it, let alone one who subscribes to Soulseek. Antonia was perhaps the only girl on Soulseek, and she had to hook up with Chaamba! Like I said, this guy was a sex magnet. And folks, Antonia was not just any girl. She was a bombshell from a wealthy, cultivated family in Chile and had a complicated story I never did comprehend. They had some chat-and-cam sex for a couple of months before Antonia came down to France to get the real thing. She stayed for a few months, then went back to Chile, then returned to France for a few months and this is how they carried on for four years, before she stopped coming to France. She was super hot.

Chaamba told me about other women who came on to him out of nowhere. Some motherfuckers had all the luck in the world. Take any book on the subject of seduction and it says that women are attracted to confident guys. That's total hogwash. In my personal experience, sexy women go for the average shy guys. Blessed are the meek, for they shall inherit the earth (and the pussy). Chaamba is living proof. Blessed also are the outright ugly guys, because French chicks seem to have a preference for that type too.

The Cosmodemonic job, on the one hand, provided me with a steady, albeit low income while I developed my radio show and expanded my free jazz network. Every evening after work, I'd search for new musicians on the web, send emails and update my playlist blog. On the other hand, the work atmosphere had been deteriorating since Rich Adams' dismissal and I often carried the tension home, which in turn caused Louise and me to fight.

On the weekends, when we were not fighting, Louise and I would go to the farmers' market for fresh food or drive to the countryside to check out the yard sales. Both of us loved buying rare old things at yard sales and the flea market. We also wandered around the city centre. We would stop by the estate agents' windows to check the properties on offer and wonder if we would ever have the money to buy something of our own. We both fantasized about living in an *angevine*-style house with a wild garden and trees in the back, and a wooden bridge leading from the first-floor balcony into the trees and beyond.

In July, another trainer quit. I hated the job too but didn't have the balls to walk away. I wanted the dole money. You get the dole if you're fired, not if you quit. I began to care less and less about work, I knew I wouldn't have to wait too long. Pretty soon, Troudecul said he had decided to fire my ass by the end of September. Exactly what I'd been looking forward to.

In the beginning of August, Louise and I took a ten-day vacation. We went to Anduze, in Auvergne in the south of France. We arrived by train and a rented car awaited us at the station. We camped at a really cheap, grassroots campsite that we found by chance. It wasn't like those tacky, commercial campsites with loads of tourists, children, swimming pool and such family fuss. Just a natural landscape with trees, bushes and an uneven terrain surrounded by woods. We drove around the area, bathed in the river, visited the magnificent underground caves, salivated at the palatial houses, ate the best onion pizza ever and got drunk on half a bottle of delicious local red wine. There is a picture of me in our photo album sitting naked on a rock in the middle of a stream, posing like Rodin's *Le Penseur*. And there's another one where I'm lying on a rock in all my naked, hirsute glory with Louise's pink summer hat hiding my manhood. Yes, we did have a fight, in a small village near Anduze, and Louise drove off abandoning me there. But she came back in ten minutes to get me.

It was one of our most memorable holidays. Of course, Louise had planned it all. When I think about it, I realize I'd probably never go anywhere if it weren't for Louise. Maybe it's because as a child I spent most of my summer holidays at home. And in college, I didn't have any money to travel and, honestly, travelling never crossed my mind in those days. I mean, where would I go in India? To me, it was an over-populated, filthy, hot expanse. Of course, I now know there's much more to India than that, but even today I find the prospect of having to make travel arrangements in India terrifying. I think I just got conditioned into being stagnant. That was another bone of contention between Louise and me. She loved to travel.

Without her I would never know these pleasures. If she didn't plan our holidays, I'd never see Venice, Lisbon, Amsterdam or the south of France. I wouldn't learn a lot of things about myself, about relationships. She made me see how selfish and self-centred I am, and explained that I need to be more generous with time and emotion if I want to cultivate real relationships. One of the ways of cherishing relationships is by giving gifts, you know, little gifts like cards, books, kitchenware and so on to family members and close friends to show them you appreciate them. Whenever we go on a holiday, Louise brings back presents for her parents, grandparents and close friends. Whereas I have a lot of trouble giving. I mean, I don't even think about bringing things back for people, and when I do, I find it very hard to decide what to give. That must be because nobody gave me anything while I was growing up. Even for my birthday, I don't remember receiving anything from my parents. As a result, I am totally insensitive to celebrating my birthday and receiving gifts. Or giving them. But I'm making improvement in that department.

I came back after the holiday refreshed and with a cooler attitude. I didn't give a fuck about work any more. To my great joy, I found a couple of occasions to put Connard and Saloppe in their place. Katrina hit New Orleans, and I continued being cool and not giving a fuck. Finally, seeing my rapidly diminishing interest in work, Troudecul relieved me of my functions fifteen days before the due date, which meant that I got paid for fifteen days without having to work.

In September, Louise got a six-month contract at CNDC, the reputed centre for contemporary dance in Angers. Around the same time, some Danish guy made cartoons of the Prophet and set off a serious controversy. I dedicated the time before the end of the year to finding ways of starting a business of my own, where I would give English conversation lessons to people in cafés. I was also fantasizing about having a jazz café of my own where I'd have all the unsung avant-garde greats come and play and I'd have enough money not to go begging for grants and shit. I'd call my café 'The Subterraneans', in homage to Jack Kerouac. I'd book whoever I liked and not give a fuck about anything. Strangely, I felt confident of being able to make it sometime in the near future. I even told my mom that I had a strong feeling I was going to pull off something big this year. Unfortunately, nothing of the sort happened.

Towards the end of the year, I connected with Anders Gronberg, a young and enterprising double bass player from Sweden. At my request, Chaamba put him up in Paris for a few nights. Anders was twenty-three then, and looked like a teenager with his tall, slender frame and long blond hair. I liked him, and at his suggestion, organized a gig for him and Yves at the American library in Angers. He stayed at our house for two days. The night I was supposed to take him to the radio studio for a live interview, we had an argument. We were in a café when I left a message on my friend Olivier's answering machine asking him to pick us up and drive us to the studio. As plan B, I suggested to Anders that if Olivier didn't show up on time we'd take a cab and split the fare.

'Why, man, if this is so much trouble let's not do it!' said Anders, looking annoyed. I asked him what he meant by that. He said I shouldn't expect him to chip in for the cab fare, he was a musician and had little money, it was my responsibility to get him to the studio, and I was already using his name and all...

Using Anders Gronberg's name! For my show! That killed me. He didn't have a fucking name. Nobody in this music had a name. And even if he did have a name, it wouldn't ring a huge bell with most people. Use his name? For what? I didn't make any money with the show, and I had interviewed better known musicians before him. And as for him spending his money, the whole time he stayed with us, we fed him and bought his drinks. He never even offered to pay for his drinks. And actually he did make some money from the gig that *I* set up for him.

Anyway, Olivier came and we did the interview. Anders left in the morning. I was disappointed in him and remained bitter for a year or so. But to give the devil his due, he is an extraordinary musician and I couldn't just tell him to go fuck himself. Over the next four years, Anders came to Angers several times, stayed at our place and played gigs. I never bought him a drink again.

Christmas was in Loches as usual. One of my presents was a crate of Bordeaux reds. Robust, full-bodied with a woody bouquet and a mellow taste. Wine is divine!

2006

17

Come New Year, I was still out of work and looking to establish my own English teaching business. After months of gathering information, I got in touch with an organization that helped new entrepreneurs start up their business. They trained them, did all the paperwork and took ten per cent of the turnover. I had several consultations with them after which I had glossy flyers printed, and distributed them myself in the mailboxes of the bourgeoisie who lived in the area around the Catho. The flyers said 'English Conversation Coaching: Speak English with Cool Confidence', and gave my contact details. Nothing happened, nobody ever called or emailed about the English lessons. I didn't know how to market the concept.

By February, the rut began to make itself felt. I had been jobless for five months, had no workable ideas and my English Conversation was dying on the vine. Every day was the same: I woke up, switched on the computer, made tea, checked email, tweaked the blog and surfed the web for jobs and business ideas. The whole day went by and I went to bed with a head full of worries, woke up the next day and repeated the cycle. I was spending a lot of time trying to figure out ways to make money on the internet. I wasn't looking for get-rich-quick schemes – or maybe I was. I sought inspiration in success stories where one brilliant idea led to unbelievable success. There are tons of success stories out there to get you feeling bad about yourself. Somebody said that success is one per cent inspiration and ninety-nine per cent perspiration. I say that one per cent is the most important element, because without it you wouldn't even know where to begin to perspire. A great idea or inspiration is like a raw diamond. Once you find the diamond, you can perspire and use your skill to cut and polish it to a desired shape and brilliance. But what will you do if you do not have the diamond? And how do you find the diamond?

Sometimes good things just happen to people without rhyme or reason. Just like bad things happen without rhyme or reason. One fine day, a million-dollar idea can pop into your head out of the blue. Or you just happen to be in the right place at the right time. Or some such serendipitous thing. Some people get incredibly lucky, just like other people get really unlucky for no reason. Conclusion: you don't find the diamond, the diamond finds you. That's what they call kismet. Fate. Destiny.

I did get a few bright ideas of my own. Like I was pretty psyched about Craigslist and wanted to start a French version of it, starting with Angers and Nantes. I got in touch with a web development agency in Angers who said they could create a Craigslist type portal for 6000 euros. Like I had that kind of dough. An independent web developer said he could do it for much less, made me court and pursue him, and finally disappeared into a black hole.

I gave up on the Craigslist idea and started a unique internet venture of my own device, the Daily Derrière blog. This was based on the entrepreneurial wisdom of turning your passion into business. Roger and I would go to the city centre with his video camera on a tripod and film the beautiful asses passing by. I put the videos on YouTube and embedded them on the blog. The idea was to make it a popular blog where ass-spotters from around the world would contribute videos of asses in motion, and I would make money with ads. It was a great idea, but it took time and I didn't know how to promote it. After making four short clips, I got tired of it and shut it down.

Napoleon Hill wrote that highly sexed people are the ones who become highly successful in life. Now, if that were true, I would be the king of Mount Moolah. I am a man haunted by sex. I'm like Woody Allen in *Deconstructing Harry*, I wanna fuck all the women I meet. The other day I wanted to fuck the job counsellor at the job office. She had big breasts and a kind face. Come to think of it, I am Woody Allenesque in so many ways. I wouldn't mind being short and ugly like him, if I had his genius as well.

The other thing that had been haunting me was the guilt of not helping my mother enough. I did send her a little money from time to time but it wasn't enough. I wanted to get her out of her lonely life in Masti and bring her to live with us. But I didn't have the financial stability to make that happen.

Going by common human experience, a bright young man of humble beginnings is supposed to rise to success and alleviate his parents' sufferings and make them proud. So why wasn't that happening to me? I mean, a little guy with big dreams should be able to make them come true. Success guru Steven Scott says that anybody who has a burning desire to succeed can make it. So what was wrong with me? I swear to God, my desire to succeed in life was burning me black on the inside. Why wasn't I getting any bright ideas, golden opportunities, perfect advice? Why didn't I have the right education, the right friends, the right environment? Why didn't I meet the right people at the right time in the right place? Why didn't I have the sense to do the right thing? Why didn't I seize the right moment? Why why WHY!

It must be my bad karma.

I must have been a rich son-of-a-bitch in my previous life, born with a silver spoon, getting laid galore, not being thankful to the Lord Almighty for life's joys. Hence, in this life, the Lord was teaching me a lesson, so that my soul would remember and in my next life would not forget to thank him for every human privilege.

By the way, in my next life, I want to be born to well-off European parents – maybe a Brit-Indian father and a French-Swedish mother. I'll live life between England, France, India and Sweden, and speak English, French, Swedish and Hindi fluently. While growing up, I'll play doctor with the neighbourhood girls, and give lots of injections. I'll study music and management. I will make love to hundreds of beautiful women of all nationalities and from all walks of life. And go on to become an entrepreneur, bridging the gap between creative music and money.

In this life, however, I was turning into a self-help junkie, thanks to all my reading and surfing the internet for ideas and inspiration. I subscribed to several newsletters on the web, by self-proclaimed, new-age, life transformation gurus who claimed to teach you how to change your life, how to make more money, how to have more sex, how to turn your whole fucking sucky life around. Once you subscribed to their newsletter, your inbox was flooded with emails carrying snippets of tricks, tips and testimonials with clickable links to buy their programs, books, CD-ROMs, teleconferences, all at a promotional price, often as generous as buy-one-get-six-free.

For a brief period, I even wanted to be a Freemason. I

thought being a member of the order would let me do more with life, but of course it was a passing fancy.

I started to have frequent shitmares – you know, nightmares about human faeces. I saw myself trying to shit but not being able to get anything out; or going to take a dump and finding the place littered with shit, with no way to get to the pot without touching shit; or feeling like I needed to shit but not being able to get up and go. Louise's little book of dream interpretation said it meant that I needed to evacuate excess baggage. I also had miserable dreams about our home in Masti. One night, I dreamt about mom, Samar and me fighting like dogs. I woke up in a sweat and felt bitter the entire day.

This year, I don't know why, I thought about Gisèle a lot. I thought about her every night and I wanted to see her again, real bad. I imagined us getting in touch by chance and rekindling the old romance.

In May, the Jazz Poetry Ensemble performed at ECU, the cultural venue for the University of Angers. I had been working on my diction, delivery and breath and was ready to give a good performance when the opportunity came. Yves assembled an interesting trio of bass, drums and sax. The drummer also doubled on the bass clarinet. The gig was great, and there was Charles McCann in the audience. We had recently reconnected.

Charles was a big fan of India and had got in touch with me through Will Pearson in 2001. He was in his early forties then, a good-looking, soft-spoken Brit with John McLaughlin looks. He used to go to India once or twice every year. We had lunch together once, and then lost touch. I had run into him in spring this year and told him about the gig at ECU. After that we met up a few more times. He had a lovely house in St Germain sur Loire which he had renovated with the help of friends. It had stone walls, beautiful floor tiles, a big fireplace, and reflected his organized and clean living. The only inconvenience was that just behind the house there was the village church with a huge bell that clanged every fifteen minutes.

Charles had made his money in the early years of his career as an IT specialist in England. Then he went to India, met a French girl in Goa and came to live in France. They separated, he stayed on.

On a sunny afternoon in June, I ran into this girl at the American library, who happened to be the ex-girlfriend of a trainee at Cosmodemonic. She was tall and sexy and I immediately wanted to get to know her in the biblical sense. Using a combination of talk and touch, I established a rapport with her in five minutes and we went for a drink. We talked for over two hours about music, hobbies, ambition, literature and all the rest of it. She loved speaking in English and dug my mannerisms. We were into each other. I offered to give her a massage. Though she laughed it away, I'm sure I would have got to second base with her had Louise not been at home. I felt my phone vibrate twice during those two hours. I didn't answer but I knew I'd better head home otherwise Louise would wonder where I was and give me hell for not answering the phone. I made an excuse, took my leave and walked back, imagining what would have happened if I didn't have to leave. We would probably have gone to another bar, maybe l'Abbaye café, and sat side by side on the sofa and after some more talk I would have found an occasion to kiss her. I got home and told Louise I had been with my friend Roger.

'You fucking idiot, listen to the message I left on your phone,' she said.

I listened to the message. In fact, when she called, my phone was accidentally answered and she had heard parts of the conversation with the girl and left a message referring to what we said about American literature. Fortunately for me, she hadn't heard the most incriminating parts. Only if I had had the sense to check messages on my cell, I would have avoided being caught lying. You can imagine what ensued. I asked her to forgive me. I said I had never lied to her before and would never lie to her again. Another lie. In a few days, we got back to normal. She loved me too much to hate me for long.

In July, a young New York bassist, Sean Beck, came to Angers with his wife, singer Janis Lurie. I set them up with Yves and they played a very nice gig in the sultry basement of T'es Rock Coco. I performed some Langston Hughes poems with the band.

That summer, Louise and I went to Lisbon. I wanted to go to Amsterdam but Louise insisted on Lisbon. I thought, Okay, I'll check out the free music scene in Lisbon. To save money, we took Eurolines, the bus service that takes you around Europe. It was a painful journey to Lisbon and back. The seats were uncomfortable, the bus was noisy, and the Jean-Claude Van Damme videos were a fucking headache. I resolved never to take Eurolines again. Lisbon was nice, but not really my kind of place. I liked the architecture but the women weren't that good-looking, though they were enticingly wide-boned below the waist. Lisbon is cheap – the cheapest capital city in Europe I've been to so far. It's even cheaper than Angers. A Bailey's coffee in a bar costs under two euros, while in Angers it costs about five, and even more in Paris.

There were tourists, but the city wasn't really happening. I was disappointed about not getting to see any avant-garde gigs or meet any of the people I knew there. They were all on holiday, the jazz places were closed for summer. We had chosen the wrong half of August to be in Lisbon.

Louise took me to the hot, shadeless, nude beaches where all you see are ugly gay men with dangling penises. I couldn't bear the heat and wanted to go back to the city but Louise wanted to enjoy the sun on the beach. Hard-headed woman. I got angry and took off. She returned after two hours and we patched up.

In September, Charles McCann called to ask if I wanted to give a few hours of English classes at ESCOM, the communication school. I said sure. Charles taught IT and English at various places in Angers and Paris, and wanted to hand over some of his classes to me, because he didn't have time for them any more. I would never have thought of approaching ESCOM for a job, because I assumed you had to have a PhD and stuff to teach at a place like that. In fact, you do need a PhD to be permanent faculty, but for a substitute English teacher's job, you only need experience and recommendation.

The job started in two days. They gave me two classes, two hours each. I was a bit intimidated by the prospect of teaching twenty-two nineteen-year-olds. I was more used to small heterogeneous groups of professional people. But I tried to do it well. Apart from teaching English grammar and vocabulary as required by the programme, I had my students make presentations on various topics, and tried to engage them in conversation in English. It wasn't easy because

French students are not used to this style of teaching, they're used to sitting passively in a language class and just jotting down what the teacher says. In mainstream French education, the only person who gets to talk in a language class is the teacher! To make matters worse, French students learn English in French. I mean, all the grammar rules are explained in French.

There were a few cute chicks in my classes who fuelled my fantasies. You know, when you're in school, you want to get into your teachers' pants, and when you become a teacher yourself, your fantasies shift to your students. Especially at ESCOM, where all you see are girls, girls, girls. Elegant, sexy girls with long legs, short skirts and the shapeliest asses in town.

Through my radio show I got in touch with John Jenkins, a great bass player from Chicago. John was also an advanced practitioner of tai chi. When we spoke on the phone, I told him I wanted to make money and do something creative with my life and needed to be pointed in the right direction to achieve this. We spoke about tai chi and its power. He said he would send me some tai chi energy through telepathy as soon as we got off the phone. I got off the phone, had dinner and went to bed. At about four in the morning, an excruciating stomach ache made me rush to the toilet. I sat in there for thirty minutes, and spent another forty minutes trying to relax my intestines and ease the pain. I emailed John asking if this was his energy working on me. He said yes, it was energy, and it had cleansed me of all the toxins in my body.

A week later, John wrote again, saying he had suffered the same painful diarrhoea in the past week. Less than a month later, I received from him a book called *Creating Money*. The book laid out in some detail exercises based on chakras and creative visualization that led to the creation of money. I tried the exercises a few times but soon gave up. I didn't believe in that mumbo jumbo.

Nothing memorable happened this year. No sex on the side, no progress in the state of life except that I wasted a lot of time trying to get a business started and eventually abandoned the idea.

We ended the year with a party at our place. The theme was 'Angels and Demons' and Louise and her friend Audrey spent hours decorating our living room to the theme. I was disguised as a little demon with golden wings and horns. Roger showed us his hilarious film, *The Hot Potato*. It was one of the best New Year's Eves ever.

2007

18

One misty morning in January, I stepped out and came face to face with a most beautiful bare bosom.

The giant billboards on Boulevard Foch boldly brandished the Cashback breasts-in-the-supermarket movie poster. I totally loved it – the poster and the fact that it was there right in the middle of the street for all to see. That's freedom of creative expression for you. *Liberté, egalité, sexualité!* It reminded me of the scandal in India caused by the python ad with Madhu Sapre and Milind Soman. That was a beautiful picture and you didn't even see any breasts.

I decided to let my mom visit us this year. I had never asked her to visit in all these years because I didn't want to face her as a loser. Plus, I thought she wouldn't be able to manage running around for the visa and all. I was an idiot, I should have invited her sooner. All a mother wants is to see her child. I sent her a sponsorship letter and money for airfare. She procured the services of a travel agent. The visa was refused. I called the embassy in New Delhi to find out why.

'We don't explain our decisions. You can apply again in three months. And there are no guarantees that the request will be accepted,' said the grumpy frog. There was nothing to do but wait and re-apply in three months' time.

Meanwhile, I enjoyed teaching at ESCOM even more this year. I was more confident as a teacher and the students were brighter and more forthcoming. And the girls were prettier. They kept my creative juices flowing. I was what I call a 'jiving teach'. I was full of enthusiasm and students liked me. We talked about new technology and watched episodes from *Sex and the City* and George Carlin shows. I was the type of language teacher the French education desperately needed. Besides, ESCOM paid an enviable hourly rate. I wished I could teach there full time, but I was just a substitute teacher, a *vacataire*, and had only six hours of classes a week, which was supplemented by my dole money. It's amazing how the education industry in France runs on manpower supplied mainly by substitute teachers. It's much cheaper to hire vacataires for a set number of hours each year than to have permanent faculty. Some people are vacataires forever and fare really well, like Pam and David. They have a set number of contracts every year. Newbies have a harder time building the network.

Now I had a foot in the door in the vacataire milieu, but my mind was elsewhere. Instead of penetrating further into the network and looking for opportunities at other schools, I was still busy looking for a business idea that would work and let me be my own boss and make me more money than I would with any job. And so life went on, worrying about everything, thinking unholy thoughts about the hot ESCOM students. I stumbled upon the audio version of *Death of a Salesman* and it made me feel even worse about myself. I identified with Biff, the unsuccessful elder brother, and went through a bout of self-pity for several weeks.

The only constantly positive thing in my life was the *Free Jazz Experience*. It gave me a reason to wake up in the morning. I loved checking the mailbox for new CDs that arrived in envelopes of varying sizes and thickness, decorated with stamps from far-off lands. The show was going great guns and was also aired on a radio in Nantes and one in Toulouse.

For a year now, Yves had been acting as artistic advisor at the ECU. I asked him to programme Mark di Milo, a great sax player from Vienna, whom I had befriended through my show. He agreed. I started to ask around if other venues were interested. You need at least two gigs to make it financially viable for a musician coming from abroad. Le Pannonica in Nantes said they were interested in Mark for May this year and I thought my dream of bringing Mark to France was finally coming true. But when the time came to finalize the project, Yves said it wasn't going to work out. He gave me some lame reason. That was a blow to me. If Yves wouldn't help me with a jazz project, who else would?

Meanwhile, a different dream came true in March. The Jazz Poetry Ensemble was booked to play at Le Pannonica. It was so unexpected. All the great American and European musicians had played on that stage, including Joe McPhee, and it fell into place with minimal effort on my part. Our drummer had run into the director of Le Pannonica and waxed eloquent about our ensemble of Beat poetry and free jazz. Coincidentally, the director had been planning something on the same lines. As part of their outreach, the Panno folks gave us a second gig, consisting of a presentation on the Beat generation and a short concert at the Uni of Nantes. I was at the top of my game. I made the audience chant Om, and opened the performance with 'Howl'. I read the first two stanzas without music. Then the bass, drums and sax joined in one by one, every two stanzas, building the intensity of the music in stages, finally bringing it to a high voltage finale by drowning out the voice. We were cookin'. There were other poems by Ginsberg and Lawrence Ferlinghetti, haikus by Kerouac and an excerpt from *On the Road*. I played little instruments here and there: different types of whistles, a toy trumpet, a blues harp and a saxophone mouthpiece. As the musicians were blowing high energy funky music, I blew soap bubbles at the audience.

It was a heady evening, the culmination of my whole being, my creativity, my love for jazz and poetry. I had come a long way. Of course I wasn't a rock star, but who wants to be a rock star? I was what I wanted to be that evening. The applause, the audience and the beautiful women made me want to be a full-time performer. I imagined that the Pannonica gig was a sign of my upward mobility in the world of jazz, and that Jack Kerouac was going to change my life like he had, apparently, Bob Dylan's. I fantasized about going around France, performing poetry and getting laid after gigs. And making money. That would be the perfect life. Music, minge and moolah!

Nothing life-changing happened, though. In the next few months, I tried to get gigs at universities and venues in other cities but nothing came of it and my enthusiasm wore off. An Italian lady, from the audience at Pannonica, emailed me a haiku that Allen Ginsberg had scribbled in her notebook when she was a child in Italy. Something about the moon, the waves and the mist.

In April this year, to the disappointment of the socially inclined and to the joy of the right-inclined French population, Nicolas Sarkozy became the twenty-third president of la République. He took over the office like a knight in shining armour who would save la France, and looked like he was going to bust some balls.

'We're going to change la France,' he said, 'we are going to make the system more efficient, we're going to cut unemployment... Look at how the English do it, look at how the Swedes do it, we can do it as well...' Seemed like he wanted to change the whole fucking country in a hurry, with quick-fix measures: curb immigration, hunt down the illegals, put 'em in jail, send 'em back to Africa. He attracted a lot of public attention and ridicule for his pompous lifestyle, and then for his new singer wife. *Guignols des Infos*, the cult TV show, portrayed him as a vacation-loving, marguerita-sipping, Rolex-wearing, short guy with a tall wife, who referred to common French folk as country bumpkins.

Mom re-applied her French visa and finally got it in May. The travel agent unscrupulously charged her hidden expenses. I would have been surprised if he hadn't. Mom flew down in June. Louise and I went to pick her up at the airport. She didn't recognize me at first. She smelled of India, phenol mixed with body odour and stale breath. We embraced and she wept. Louise wept as well. I was just embarrassed. We took the train home and had lunch together.

The next morning, as mom and I were having tea, Louise woke up and came over to kiss me. When I resumed sipping my tea, mom said, 'It's all superficial here. Even the way you kiss is superficial. In India they kiss with feeling and emotion.'

I didn't know how to respond to this ridiculously opinionated observation. She had just arrived in the country, had seen nothing of it and knew nothing of the culture, yet she pronounced a judgement on how we kissed and how superficial we were. I was tempted to ask if she had ever seen anybody kiss in India, but I just pressed my lips and nodded my head.

Other than that, we got along most of the time, but when we went to Louise's grandparents' house, mom and I had the most unpleasant encounter. At dinner, I had a little disagreement with mom, after which she didn't speak much for the rest of the meal. After dinner, when I was helping to clear the table and got ready to do the dishes, mom followed me into the kitchen and asked, 'Why are *you* doing the dishes?'

'Who else will do it?' I said.

'Oh god!' she sighed and went to her room. I started doing the dishes but felt like something was not right. When I went to check on mom I found her sitting on the side of the bed, sobbing. I sat down, put my arm around her and asked her what was wrong.

'Is it because I spoke to you badly? I'm sorry. I won't treat you like that again.'

'Why are *you* doing the dishes?' she asked. 'If you do that in order to be able to stay here, come back home with me.' I remained quiet, startled by this observation.

'What will I say to your mama?' she continued. 'That you wash dishes here?'

I was getting super annoyed but didn't react. 'I'm just being useful, I'm helping our hosts. Don't people do that in India?'

'No, in India, the son-in-law is not supposed to help with the chores,' she retorted.

My patience was running thin.

'But this is not India, it's not the same equation. Here, the son-in-law is a member of the family like any other. They treat me so well, they cook what I like, they're being so good to you. I don't have to lift a finger here, the least I can do to show some respect is clear the table and do the dishes, just like I do at home with Louise. It's the culture here, everybody contributes. You have to open up your mind. You say go back with you. Go back to what? To your one-room house? To Masti, to that miserable life of nothing? My life is here and I live it like it should be lived...'

Then I went back to the kitchen and continued to do the dishes. Though I believed in what I said to her, I felt weird doing the dishes alone now. I asked Louise to do the wiping while I did the washing. Mom's observation had left its mark, I don't know why. Was it due to my own insecurities about my place in the world? On my next few visits to Louise's parents' or grandparents', I avoided doing the dishes.

We took mom to the festival of oriental music in Saint-Florent-le-Vieil. She loved the song and dance performance and tried to translate the Hindi songs for Louise. Later, Louise's parents took mom to Château de Montsoreau for a performance of the operetta in which her father sang. I stayed home to get some time alone. Mom enjoyed the performance, drank a glass of bubbly and said it tasted like lemonade. There, she spotted a woman who looked like Helen, the Bollywood vamp of yore, and got all excited. Louise had to take her to talk to the woman.

When we were back in Angers, I took mom shopping, and we ran into Léa. She was this beautiful friend of mine whom I desperately wanted to fuck. She had a tattoo on her lower back. Tattoo or no tattoo, I don't think I've ever been friends with a girl without longing to befriend her private parts. Anyway, Léa asked mom how she liked France and mom said she didn't like it. That was embarrassing. After having a good time here for weeks, she still said she didn't like it. She would spill inanities like, 'Here everybody is a stranger. Back in India everybody feels like you know them.' What can you say to that?

Despite the occasional tiffs, my mother and I had a pleasant time. We talked about a lot of things, life here and life there. She cooked us Indian food. Two delicious months. She entertained me with stories about our relatives in India. She also told me how Samar had paved his own path to Australia six years ago. He decided where he wanted to study and asked mama for help with the bank loan. Mama introduced him to the loan officer in the Bank of Punjab in Masti. It was the first time anyone had requested the loan officer of that little bank for a loan of seven lakh for studying abroad. Samar provided the officer with all the info and helped him with the paperwork. To speed up the process, the two of them went together to the bigger branch of the bank in Lucknow. By the time Samar obtained the loan, everyone in the Masti and Lucknow branches knew him by name and spoke of him in admiration. I was doubly proud of my brother when I heard this. Why didn't he tell us the story when he visited us?

Mom loved Louise and said I was lucky to have found a girl like her, that I must have given away pearls in my previous life to have such luck, that it was a wonderful thing I had not married an Indian girl, because an Indian girl would never leave me alone and would nag me to insanity. I agreed. Louise and mom got along really well and developed a language of their own – a mix of broken English, French, Hindi and gestures. I had refused to be the interpreter early on.

To my consternation, sometime during her stay, mom hinted not so subtly at our having kids. It's a topic that comes back to us frequently. I know Louise's clock is ticking, and though I agree it's great to have children when you're young, I still need to grow up and stand on my feet before I am comfortable with the idea of becoming a father. I don't want to have children until I'm absolutely certain I'll be able to provide for them in every possible way. I want to raise my children with a winner mindset and I want them to be proud of their dad and look up to me. I want my children to be free, free in mind, free from fear of failure, and pursue whatever they desire and go all the way. I want them to pursue their dreams knowing that they can fall back on their dad. Knowing that you can afford to fail is a guarantee of success in the long term.

So, you see, having children is a huge responsibility and I obviously don't have the shoulders for it right now.

There were no more classes at the university after May, and I had no income at all. Beginning July, I took up the job of night receptionist at a hotel. After the hotel job in 2001, I had decided never to go back to a night job. But I didn't have a choice, I had been unemployed too long. Mom was there and expenses had risen. It was a terrible job, very tiring. All the work one had to do in that hotel! Apart from the usual check-in, check-out, the tasks included vacuum cleaning the floor, setting the tables for breakfast, throwing out the empty bottles and filing the paperwork for the day. On top of that, I had to be the bartender as well. Many times, while on the job, I felt a surge of regret and shame. If my mom knew what I had to do to make a measly income, it would break her heart.

Mom left in the first week of August. She wept all the way to the airport and on the plane. Later she told me that she showed off her French to the air-hostess by saying *bonjour, comment ça va?* The next weekend, Louise tried her hand at cooking paratha. Although it looked like a mutilated starfish, it tasted just fine.

The school year started in September and I went back to giving classes at ESCOM, but kept the hotel job for a few more months. In December I quit to take up a part-time call centre job. The banking department of the French postal service was trying to establish its identity as a bank, and it had a new website. My job was to take calls from customers and explain how the website worked, how to get a new password, how to clean cookies, which browser to use and so on. It was a shitty job.

By October, Yves had another reason for not bringing Mark di Milo to play in Angers. This year, he himself played majority of the jazz gigs at ECU, including two gigs with Sean Beck and Janis Lurie. Yves was displaying typical musician behaviour. Now that he had found a place where he could play as much as he wanted, make some money and have friends play there, who would return the favour by including him in gigs at other venues, he was going to do just that. He was not going to give a fuck about me. It was the only time that I had asked him for help on a project that he had the power to make happen. He knew how much I wanted it but chose to ignore my request. He also ignored the fact that I had brought him some nice gigs in the recent past.

Ironically, the French government proved to be more gracious than Yves. They granted me citizenship. I had first applied in early 2006, following which Louise and I were called in for individual in-depth interviews with a police officer who typed out every word we said. I was also summoned to the *préfecture*, where they asked me to write in French why I wanted to become a French citizen. I had written one sentence: I think it's natural to want to be a citizen of the country where I want to spend the rest of my life.

Mom had to run around the municipality of Masti to get a copy of my birth certificate with her name on it. It was finally made possible through mama's intervention. Dad had to bribe some low-level police officers to get my police clearance. All the trouble paid off finally. Acquiring French citizenship was the final confirmation of permanent freedom. And I was lucky. Soon afterwards, the Sarko administration tightened the laws concerning immigration and naturalization.

I wanted to spend New Year's Eve at our place, as usual, but Louise wanted to celebrate with new people for a change. Some people she knew only slightly had invited her to celebrate the New Year at a bar. The guests were supposed to bring something light to eat, and contribute twenty euros each towards dinner. I had my misgivings about celebrating the New Year with strangers, but my wife accused me of being narrow-minded and not wanting to make an effort for her sake. So I gave in, against my better judgement. And whaddyaknow, it turned out to be the most fucking rotten New Year's Eve we have ever had. The bar was a seedy joint, the people were uninteresting middle-aged losers and the dinner was greasy and tasteless. Worst New Year's Eve ever.

2008

19

I hadn't yet recovered from the shock of Benazir Bhutto's assassination, which occurred at the end of the previous year, when Heath Ledger died. He had everything – beauty, talent, money, sex – but not enough time. Meanwhile, millions of insignificant losers out there have all the time in the world to live their small cockroach lives and copulate and increase their tribe.

That's what we do, we lesser mortals. We breathe, eat, fuck and die. We come and go like flies, creatures of utmost insignificance. Only a chosen few leave a mark. I was sick of being a common nobody. Sick of riding the same trains as millions of other nobodies, going to the same shops, wearing the same brands, sharing with them the same low level of life, without distinction, without achievement, just a cog in a gigantic wheel. I was sick of living in this country of poor, unemployed, overworked, underpaid people. I was sick of being one of them. I wanted to rise above all those unfortunate common idiots. I wanted to live a life where money is no object. I wanted to be in a different social milieu, rub shoulders with the glitterati. Create something of value. I wanted life to rock 'n' roll. I wanted to do more. I wanted to be more.

I emailed Yves once again, urging him to do something about bringing Mark to Angers. He did not reply. I decided not to ask him again and wait until I could pay him back in the same coin. One day I would have my own jazz café, with its walls lined with vintage paperbacks. I would also set up a free jazz ashram, where people would come in search of peace and pleasure and indulge in *Eyes Wide Shut* type orgies to the sounds of free jazz. Wouldn't that be something? Free jazz and free love!

To spice up my social life, I started an English-speaking social club in Angers. I created a website and promoted it through flyers and web forums. Quite a few people signed up. I organized meetings at Cercle Rouge, the wine bar. It was good fun and I hoped to turn it into a business someday and charge a membership fee. Thanks to the club, Laurie and I began to see each other regularly. When it was just the two of us, we'd talk about women and relationships and bitch about life and work.

One evening, Laurie and I went to hear this band, Riding the Dandy, fronted by this redhead girl I used to know at uni. Their music was pretty good and she sang in a beautiful voice. She looked much better than before. Her hair was longer, her face was radiant, she was graceful and she had one hell of an ass! I looked at her and then I looked at myself. She was up there swinging, swaying and touring with her band and here I was, the same nobody chump I used to be. Just another moment to touch base with the loser inside me.

Louise had been constantly looking for work ever since her contract with CNDC ended. It was a difficult time for her. In February she finally found a job in Chartres, at an organization that promoted dance education in schools. She was in charge of communication and public relations. She rented a small studio and moved to Chartres. She came to Angers on weekends and I went to Chartres a few times. Soon, she realized the job was far from ideal. The association was fraught with internal problems, lawsuits and incompetence. Even though she was not enthralled with the job, it was a permanent contract and it was in her chosen field, and a permanent job in France is a sort of blessing.

I hated the thought of having to leave Angers, but it was evident that I would have to move to Chartres eventually. We could not continue the relationship long distance, plus the expense of paying for two apartments was too high.

June arrived and Yves Saint Laurent departed. Samar called and said he had found the love of his life and was going to marry her in December. He had been steadily climbing the corporate ladder and somewhere on his yearly visits to Chandigarh, he had met Mona. After four years of romancing through emails, long-distance calls and annual visits, he had popped the question. They wanted a simple and quick wedding, but Mona's family wanted fanfare. So it was going to be a real Indian wedding, albeit on a smaller scale.

I had my private reservations about the union, but if Samar was happy, who was I to complain? My parents were a little worried, though. Apparently, an NRI boy getting married to an Indian girl was risky business. Every other day, the news had stories of NRI boys' families being persecuted by the police and the media. According to my parents, NRI persecution was as common today as dowry deaths were twenty years ago. I wanted to speak to Samar about this but didn't have the balls. Mom did speak to him and he was furious – he accused her of casting doubts on his future happiness.

It was clear that my brother intended to marry this girl and there was no way he would give it a second thought. He decided not to let mom and dad meet his future in-laws to avoid any complications, but dad said that he wouldn't go to the wedding without getting to know the girl's family first. So he met Mona's family and discovered that they were lovely people. Mom only spoke to them over the phone. She never could let go of her reservations, and finally said that she had placed the situation in the hands of God.

I wasn't going to attend the wedding at first – I cannot deal with all the relatives and the drama – but Louise said it was important I go. Even mom and dad insisted I go. Thank god they drilled sense into me – how could I even imagine missing my only brother's wedding! Finally Louise and I decided to go together. She bought the tickets online and we were all set to arrive in Chandigarh five days before the wedding in December.

In August, Louise and I went to a small village in Sweden, where Anders Grönberg had organized a charming little festival of music, poetry and food. The performances took place in the barn of his parents' house by the river. I could picture myself living in a house like that, built of wood and painted in red, with big glass windows, concerts in the barn and two little cabins for my parents. We slept in a tent in the garden behind the red house. The music was great, the food delicious, and the girls were beautiful.

We went to Stockholm from there and stayed in Anders's apartment for a few days. We also visited Uppsala, Falun, Leksand and Talleberg, and stayed on campsites. I loved the Swedish churches – narrow rectangles with high pointed spires. And the most surprising thing about Swedish churches is that they have toilets!

Sweden is an expensive country, with shitty weather. It rained the whole time. In Uppsala, it rained so hard I was afraid it would tear our tent apart. Uppsala is a university town very much like Angers and the young people there were very polite. Every time we stopped someone to ask for directions they apologized for the weather. And we got lucky with people a couple of times. In a cute little café in Talleberg, the waitress was so happy to meet us that she charged us for less than half the bill. Another time, a bus driver gave us a free ride. He was English and was delighted to meet an English-speaking Indian from France.

The Swedish girls, *svenska flickoor*, looked at me lovingly, they seemed open and willing to talk and I got the feeling I would have had a successful sex life in the land of the Vikings. And to refute a cliché, not all Swedish babes are tall blondes with blue eyes. In fact, the ratio of tall blondes and not-so-tall brunettes seemed to be fifty-fifty. *Jag Alsker Sverige!*

After the holidays, we had to plan my move to Chartres. Though it was a frightening thought at first, by September, I had come round to the idea of leaving Angers. I felt there wasn't anything left for me there any more. I had been sending out my CV to other schools and to the university for more work but I hadn't heard back from anyone. Besides, I was sick of the same ol' same ol' of Angers. The same streets, same people, same stagnation, same fuckin' everything. Maybe being stuck in Angers was what kept me stuck in the rut. It was time for a change, I needed to move on.

'Everything happens for the best. Let's feel the fear and do it anyway,' I said to myself and began to look for jobs in Chartres and Paris – Paris is just an hour's train ride from Chartres.

Finally, I heard back from a reputed language school in Paris. At the interview, the recruitment manager asked me how come I spoke with an American accent. I told him that my dad had lived in the US in his youth, had acquired the accent and passed it on to me. That, of course, is bullshit, I didn't want to say I had picked it up from movies, people and endless hours of talking to myself in different voices. And honestly, it is not American, just Americanish.

After a week-long teacher-training in September, I was hired to work at their language centre in Versailles. Now that I had a job, we started looking for an apartment in Chartres. In the meantime, I stayed with Louise in her tiny studio. We still had our apartment in Angers and my workdays were divided between Angers and Versailles. It was a hectic schedule with a lot of trains to ride. I taught in Angers on Monday and Tuesday afternoons. On Tuesday evening, I caught the train back to Chartres. From Wednesday to Saturday, I worked in Versailles. I had to wake up really early to get to work in Versailles and got back home only around nine or ten in the evening. The morning train to Versailles was jam-packed with commuters, reminding me of the local train in Bombay.

On the train, I would read, sleep and daydream. I tried to visualize the big wooden house with a barn, my parents inside their cabins. I fantasized about going around the world reading poetry, making frequent trips to Samar in Sydney, loving my redhead student and such pleasurable thoughts. Daydreams aside, the reality of the situation was that I was being fucked by the French railways. It's so goddamn expensive to travel by train in this country, it's almost cruel. I got creative and found ways not to buy tickets every time I boarded the train.

In the middle of October, I gave up the apartment in Angers and we moved into a bigger apartment near the train station in Chartres. It was a nice apartment with large windows, a lot of light and a view of the neighbour's garden. Louise missed the terrace we had in Angers – we couldn't have terrace parties any more. But that was okay, for we didn't have any friends here. We painted the bedroom silver.

At first I enjoyed working at the language centre. My colleagues were nice, they were mostly women. And very often you got to have free lunch with the trainees. The trainees were really interesting people – mostly business executives. There was this gentleman who held a high position at Lloyd's bank in Paris. He was funny and loved to relate stories about his life: his friends were rich, influential people who owned and raced boats; his wife was small and beautiful; his son had a sexy girlfriend of Swedish-Finnish blood; as a young banker, he had once been kissed by a beautiful client; his surgeon friend was sleeping with a nurse... you know, such inside stories.

Some very attractive women, young and not so young, crossed my path as well. There was an accountant who worked for a huge medical equipment company, and loved *Desperate Housewives*. There was a beautiful young aerospace engineer. There were others. I didn't get much time to develop anything with any of them. The manager, this crazy woman called Madame Lethon, started sending me to the centre in St Sulpice, which she managed as well. St Sulpice was out of my way, and meant a much more complicated train route. Some of the other staff members who knew my situation concurred that Lethon was taking advantage of me. I decided not to take this shit. On December 1, I wrote a polite email requesting Lethon not to send me to St Sulpice any more. Two days later I found myself opening a registered letter informing me that they had decided to terminate my employment at the end of the three-month trial period.

I wasn't really surprised by the firing, I had sort of seen it coming. Even when I started there, I knew I was not going to stay long. It was just another exploitative, dead-end job. But I needed it in order to make the shift from Angers to Chartres. What surprised me was how promptly they had me fired, as though they were eagerly waiting for the opportunity. I called Lethon and she said, yes, she had to let me go because I was not flexible enough, and yes, my email was 'the drop that made the glass overflow'. That's French for 'the last straw on a camel's back'.

Like Will Pearson once stated the universal truth ever so eloquently in his posh London accent, 'Anybody who operates a language school is, without exception, a cunt.'

20

I was going back home after nine years. I was full of apprehension. I hadn't gone back all this time, first, because I just didn't want to go back, not even temporarily, to everything that I had left behind. Second, I had nothing to show for myself. I had no money and I had achieved nothing. I didn't want my parents to feel bad about my non-achievement. Personally, I didn't mind telling the truth about my situation, but my father wouldn't like it. He called and said it was nice that I had decided to go for the wedding, but what was I going to tell people about my life in France? I said, I was going to tell the truth, that I was just managing to survive. He said if I talked like that it would ruin his reputation in the family. He had told everybody that I was doing very well in France.

Louise and I arrived in New Delhi in the second week of December, in the wee hours of the morning. Samar and

Mona picked us up. It was fantastic seeing my brother again and Mona was a beautiful, happy girl. On our way to Mona's apartment in South Ex, Samar and I laughed hysterically, remembering stories from the past. When we reached home, we had Taj Mahal tea, I telephoned my friend Balbir and then we all went to bed. Balbir came over in the afternoon. We talked, and he sang us a couple of Jagjit Singh ghazals. Louise slept on in the other room.

Samar accompanied us to Chandigarh the next day. I was afraid of catching the train alone with Louise. I wouldn't know where to go and what to do. And I was right. When we entered New Delhi Railway Station, the sight of a million people swarming like ants all over the place scared me. I felt like a foreigner in my own country.

Samar's best friend Prayag met us at the Chandigarh station. Back in the day, Prayag used to come to our place in Sector 11 and make us chai. He took us to dad's place. My cousin Ragmeet came to see us right after our arrival. Ragmeet is four years my junior but we were close in high school. His daddy never owned a car either. We used to go to sweet shops in Mohali to have pastries and jalebis, taking turns to treat each other. He gave me a card when I was leaving India, telling me how bad he felt. The best thing about Ragmeet was that he outdid us all when it came to the sex game. In high school, he was busted with his pants down in the company of his then girlfriend, by her brother. Rags was ragging the rooster at a time when most older boys were taking matters in their own hands.

Today, Rags has a good IT job, a gorgeous IT wife, a daughter, and he takes care of his parents. An ideal man. Amazing how different people with the same set of circumstances produce different results, how some people go and get what they want while others sit and complain about what they haven't.

We visited my cousin Veena and her husband JK at their hotel. Five years ago, JK quit his high-paying bank job and launched this hotel. It was a roaring success. Veena ran a women's wear boutique. Their daughter Lisa was studying to be a dentist. Their son Johar had studied engineering in Canada and now worked in London.

While we were having aperitif, JK gave me a sidelong glance, sizing me up. Then he asked what I was doing in France. His tone said, 'I know you're not up to much, but I'm asking for the sake of conversation.' Or 'confirmation'. I said I taught English at the university. There were other cousins-once-removed present. They were all in their early twenties now and had all travelled to London, New York, Singapore, Paris. They only wore branded clothing. I did not feel comfortable among them. They talked like teenagers – been there, seen this, done that – typical Indian rich kid talk. I still didn't fit. The food at the hotel was delicious, but I had lost my appetite.

The next day, we went to see Mona's family and met her parents and her sister Kirti. Kirti was involved in theatre, and did some copywriting work. We clicked right from the start. During our entire stay in Chandigarh, she flirted with me and I encouraged her, much to Louise's displeasure and scorn. In fact, I think if Louise hadn't been around, I would have found a way to go all the way with Kirti, even though screwing your younger brother's sister-in-law is not the done thing in India. I didn't give a fuck, I was an outsider. Why shouldn't I give into a little temptation and bring some excitement to my dreary life? Louise knew what I was up to and told me not so subtly that she understood the game I was playing with Kirti, and that I was not a teenager and ought to know better and behave accordingly. But I was not listening. I was determined to enjoy my trip and the wedding as much as I could. I told her to enjoy the wedding atmosphere with an open mind and to stop complaining.

The next day, we picked mom up from the Chandigarh bus station. She was very happy to be united with Louise and cast a scrutinizing glance at Mona. Samar had booked her a room at JK's hotel. My dear friend Manish arrived the same evening, from Dubai. He had put on weight. His face had gone from chiselled to round and fleshy. But his attire and manner retained their elegance and charm. His arty Tom Ford shades added to his creative dude aura.

I don't exactly remember how I met Manish but it must have been at DAV college, through common friends. We were good friends for some time, then we had an argument and stopped talking. Rather, I stopped talking to him. He made a few attempts to communicate which I rejected. We patched up eventually, before he joined AEISEC. Then Manish rented a room in the same house as mine. We would go everywhere on my little Priya scooter before he bought a second-hand Yezdi and baptized it *fille de joie*, lady of pleasure, at my suggestion. He would tell me about the hip parties and the European students he got to meet through AEISEC. Once, on an AEISEC trip, Manish gave a massage to a couple of Estonian chicks. They took turns getting into his bed and my bony friend massaged them in the quiet of the night. I felt very envious and imagined two pairs of white, smooth, fleshy thighs entwined with Manish's brown, hairy ones. But the envy cooled down when I heard that neither girl fucked him. That must have been the most serious boner-bust of anybody's life!

In the days preceding the wedding, we went out with cousins and friends to noisy cafés and restaurants, where we drank a lot and shouted to get ourselves heard. I kissed all the young girls. I said I'm French, and in France we kiss. They were all amused and offered me their cheeks. I think they found me a bit exotic with my gracious French wife. I spoke Hindi to my heart's content and avoided Hinglish.

My suit was stitched in three days and I went shopping for shirts, ties and shoes. They did not have my size in shirts and the designs conformed to the Indian taste, not mine. Finally, I decided to borrow Samar's shirts and ties. They were one size too large but I managed.

Mama came for the wedding and stayed at JK's hotel. He let me inspect the three holes in his back caused by gunshots inflicted upon him by a robber who wanted his gold chain and money. After taking three shots, mama had emptied his own Webley & Scott into the motherfucker and sent him straight to hell. Served him right to fuck with mama.

The wedding ceremony took place in the gurudwara. Samar wore a shiny grey suit and a light pink turban. Manish took a lot of pictures with his wide-angle lens Canon. Right after the ceremony, we drove over to a wedding complex on the outskirts of Chandigarh, where the reception was being held.

There was a Punjabi DJ with a dhol, entertaining the guests. I kept my distance. My brother's friends had come down from Dubai, Sydney and Singapore. I couldn't think of any of my friends who would do that for me. I didn't have any friends. The ones I did were losers, just like me. Birds of a feather.

The morning after the wedding, Manish had to leave for Delhi. We went for breakfast to the DAV college canteen for old times' sake. I went to look at the library. It hadn't changed at all. The attendants looked exactly as they had twelve years ago. The heavy, rectangular wooden desks and chairs were the same. Pierre Jeanneret had designed those, and they would fetch thousands of dollars in the international market. I had spent a lot of time here reading, dreaming and fantasizing about playing footsie with a tootsie. In my time, it used to be a boys-only college. Back at the hotel, Veena and JK grilled mom to find out what we had got from Mona's family. They refused to believe it was a wedding sans dowry. Samar was strictly against dowry.

On the afternoon of December 23, I had an argument with mom in her hotel room. A bad, bad argument. I had been very irritated by her habit of talking too much, all the time – she did not even let me have a conversation. Every time someone asked me a question, she would respond. I thought she would stop after a few times, but she didn't, so I started telling her off every time she butted in. This time, she had said something to Louise that irritated me. When Louise went to change, I snubbed mom. She made a disgusted face and said, 'I'd rather stay in Masti or die than be near you. You snub me every time I open my mouth.'

'That's because you open your mouth too much. you never let me talk to people in peace, you're always answering for me. I am fed up of you. You weren't like this when you came to France.'

We began to argue, loudly and bitterly. Her tone brought back memories of when she punished me as a kid or said cruel things to me back in Masti, memories of all that I hated about my childhood, all that I was ashamed of, and all that I had wanted to get away from. And I lost it at the deepest level.

'Shut the fuck up, you stupid bitch. I hate you. And let me tell you the truth, all that I hate about India is *you*, I wanted to leave the country because I wanted to get away from you.'

She fell completely silent. After a few minutes she left the room without a word. I sat down, seething. She returned after two hours and announced that she had made a reservation to leave for Masti the next day, and that she was not going to go to Amritsar with us. Louise had been in the bathroom during our argument, but she figured that something serious had gone down. She tried to persuade mom to stay but she refused to budge. Louise and I took her to the station the next day. There was still tension in the air but I was already feeling sorry about the fight, and saying goodbye to mom was hard. What I had said to her was cruel, but it had to come out. I knew we would soon forgive and forget and resume our usual relationship.

December 24 was very quiet. No lights, no celebration, no roast turkey, no wine, no presents. Louise and I went to Backpackers Café for a quiet coffee. On Christmas day, we set out for Amritsar in a hired car, the newly-weds and our parents, minus mom. On the way, Samar and I sang the Hindi film songs we had grown up with. He told us how hard he had worked in Australia while he was studying. He had worked in department stores and on the docks in Sydney, along with attending classes, some days running on barely four hours sleep. We visited the Golden Temple, had langar and started on our journey back. It was a most dangerous drive as the road was covered in dense fog and everything was invisible. But we made it back safely around midnight.

The next day I went to see Kirti to chat about her copywriting work. She looked tantalizing with her shiny shoulder-length hair, green panties peeking out of the waist of her jeans, a tight t-shirt, short enough to show off her hip tattoo. I was surprised to see that – things really had changed since I left India. Girls didn't wear clothes like that ten years ago, certainly not in Chandigarh, let alone get tattoos.

After our copywriting conversation, Kirti started getting ready for another appointment in town. I stood at the door of her bedroom while she brushed her hair. I said, Show me your tattoo. She, in her usual coquettish manner, lifted her t-shirt a bit to reveal the artwork. I asked her to come closer. She came closer and lifted the t-shirt again. I wanted to touch the tattoo and kiss her there. I considered it for two seconds – imagining myself kissing the tattoo, grabbing her ass, cupping her breasts, the tension rising, blood rushing to fill the veins around my organ. But I didn't want to be caught by my brother's mother-in-law in the act of groping his sister-in-law. The unscrupulous bastard in me just didn't have the balls. So I just looked at the tattoo and said, 'Uh huh, interesting,' as if it were some specimen. We got out of the house, caught an auto-rickshaw to Sector 9, where she had the appointment. I walked the rest of the distance to the hotel, stopping to buy samosas on the way.

The next day we took the train to Agra. On the train, the ticket collector said that we were on the waiting list. What the fuck did that mean? You pay for your journey and on the train they say you don't have a seat. That alone put me off travelling in India. I had to grease the ticket collector's palm to get us a seat. Agra was filthy as hell but Louise loved the Taj Mahal. The entrance to the Taj cost me twenty rupees but it cost her 750 rupees, the special fee for foreign tourists. People stared at her.

Louise loved India but she hated the stares. It's amazing how people can stand in your face and stare into it without blinking. The hotel where we spent the night was creepy and squalid and too expensive for what it was – the bedsheets were stained and the bathroom was like in a nightmare. We didn't have time to look for a better one. I enjoyed going around the market with Louise, looking to buy a small statue of Ganesha. Our train from Agra to Delhi was delayed indeterminately, and we had to spend eight hours at the station, watching street children beg the shit out of white tourists. I shooed them away in Hindi when they approached Louise. I joked with a beggar girl saying I had no money and that she should give me some and she actually extended her hand to give me her coins.

We finally reached Delhi early the next morning and got a taxi to Balbir's place in Gurgaon. Balbir and I had become friends at boarding school. I hated the school and I've never forgiven my dad for sending Samar and me there. It was a far cry from the hip boarding schools I saw on TV shows and read about in books. The boys at this school literally – and I do mean literally – thrust their finger up your ass for fun. I remember Samar crying uncontrollably one day, saying he didn't want to stay there any more, and I felt so helpless for not being able to help my little brother. Thankfully, at the end of the second month, dad took him back to Masti to finish class seven and eight at St Joseph's. But I had to stay on at Five Rivers, I had no choice. Dad had already paid the yearly fees for tuition, board and lodging at Five Rivers for both of us, and if we both left, that money would be entirely wasted. So I had to spend four years within those barbed wire walls. The most depressing time of my life.

The founder, owner, director and principal of the school was this mean Sikh guy who reminded me of Saddam Hussein. He exuded power and menace. Once, in class twelve, I was standing by the notice board when I saw him walking down the corridor, and I wished him good afternoon. 'What have you done to your beard?' he said, and landed a heavy slap in my face. Then he dragged me by the arm into his office and slapped me some more and pushed me so I fell. The tyrant would have gone on with the beating had he not been interrupted by a staff member. That fucker had taken the liberty to punish me for the sin of trimming my beard, because it went against the Sikh religion. Another time, the bastard had dragged a girl out of the girls' hostel by her hair. Her crime was that she was going out with a guy, and no gender mixing was allowed after classes. I mean, corporal punishment was pretty common in India, but that guy was out of bounds.

My friends in other boarding schools had fun. I envied Rahul, who studied at the prestigious Lawrence Public school in Sanavar. Kipling's Kim studied there. I was an unlucky kid, born in a shitty country, in a shitty town, to middling, loveless parents and went to the shittiest school on the planet.

Nonetheless, at Five Rivers, I was popular with the teachers. Not only was I an active student, I also did a wonderful Dev Anand impersonation. Everybody called me Dev Anand or just Dev. I think it was Dev Anand, along with Balbir, who got me through that bad phase safely.

Balbir and I met in the dining hall not long after my arrival. He looked like the Sikh boy in the hip boarding school on TV. He was in class nine and only a year older than I was. He had a toned, muscular body and was strong and quick. He had practised martial arts briefly. Many a time, he protected me from bullies. He was like an elder brother. He talked to me when I was down, which happened quite frequently. He taught me how to sing Kishore Kumar songs. We went out together when we could, and talked for hours. A few times, we had big arguments and stopped talking to each other, but he always took the first step towards reconciliation. We lost touch after high school and reconnected after college, then lost touch again when I came to France. Reconnected in 2005. He said he described me to his friends as a person who had followed his dreams.

And got stuck in a celestial traffic jam, I thought.

We stayed with Balbir and his wife for two nights. We wrestled arms. I won with my right, he won with his left. Our flight back was delayed by several hours due to the fog, so the airline offered us a delightful breakfast of puri-sabzi at the airport. We hadn't eaten puri for our entire stay and there it was.

As I sat in the airport terminal, staring at the planes parked outside, I looked back on my holiday. This time, I looked at India with European eyes. And I loved everything. I thought the girls in Chandigarh were beautiful and the people were friendly. It is an exotic country for a vacation if you don't mind the squalor, train delays and bumps in the roads. Louise and I were struck by the beauty and genuine smiles of the street children. I had never noticed these things while I lived there. I was also surprised to see how much money people had today. Young professionals could afford to spend much more than they could in my time. Everybody seemed to have the latest model of cell phone and phone calls were cheap. The restaurants, cafés and shops had uniformed guards to open the door for you. The new fast-food joints were great. Unlike France, here they were squeaky clean and elegant, and the food was excellent. And all the bakeries had this sinfully delicious Black Forest cake. The best value for money in India was still the food.

2009

21

On the flight back, I daydreamed about starting a hip international jazz-blues-folk festival in India, with Manish on the communications front, Balbir on logistics and yours truly as creative director. I returned to Chartres to several inches of snow and a heightened sense of worthlessness. The unbearable insignificance of my being gnawed at me more than ever. All my cousins and friends were out there in the real world with real skills, working worthwhile jobs and carving out a rich life for themselves. I couldn't even make a decent monthly salary.

In the first week, I called mom and we apologized to each other. 'You're my mother and I am your son and that's how it will always be, no matter how much we fight,' I told her. At the end of January, the Jazz Poetry Ensemble played at the fine arts museum in Angers. I wore my red Fab India kurta. The gig was good but it did not cheer me up. I still felt worthless.

I registered at the employment office in Chartres and started looking for another English teaching job in Paris and realized that being in Chartres I was too far from Paris to be useful to any of the English language schools there. That I had managed to get a job at the language centre last year was a miracle.

Both Louise and I hated living in Chartres. It was gloomy, sad and windy. The architecture was creepy and the surrounding countryside flat and uninspiring. Chartres was just 80 km from Paris but the train took over an hour to get there, stopping at every little godforsaken station in between. I didn't go to Paris for a lot of gigs because I was put off by the thought of the creepy train ride. I didn't dig the people in Chartres either. They were ugly and had zero sense of style.

Louise had her job to keep her occupied, while I sat at home and got really depressed. To alleviate the gloom in my heart, I decided to visit my friend Leo Wiplinger in Budapest. Before leaving, I got in touch with Mark di Milo in Vienna. Mark put me in touch with Beko Grof, a fantastic sax player from Budapest, who invited me to read poetry with his band. So on the first evening in Budapest, Leo and I went to Jelen, a smoky club owned by a Dutch trombone player in the heart of the city. I had a delicious chicken salad on the house, and performed poetry with top-notch Hungarian improvisers. They hadn't thought of getting me a microphone, so I had to shout out the words. A beautiful Hungarian lady in the audience said that my performance of Langston Hughes' 'Fire' transported her to an underground club in New York!

Leo lived in the centre of Budapest and earned his bread teaching French to Hungarian executives. In his line of work, he crossed paths with loads of sexy women, and some of them didn't mind crossing the line. Lucky Leo.

Budapest is an interesting city with beauty and ugliness standing side by side, testifying to its communist past. Aside from the magnificent historical monuments, it is a city of pre-war, soot-soaked buildings with broken façades. They look like they will fall apart any day. Any structure that can stand is covered in graffiti. The night life is great, and the cafés and clubs are housed in spooky abandoned buildings, warehouses, erstwhile factories and schools. Leo took me to many of these subterranean places. We would be walking in a dark street and suddenly he would stop at the entrance of an ugly building, and we would go in. Inside, there would be a bar and sexy girls. We'd go a little further, pass through another door and there would be another bar with a different decor. Then we'd go up the stairs and find a third bar and more sexy women... If we went to the other wing of the building, there would be another bar... It was fantastic, I had never seen anything like it before.

At one such club, in an abandoned school building, there was a band playing fanfare-style music. The trumpet player was a girl with rounded features. She was average looking but I dug her body and the way she held her instrument. Just looking at her with the trumpet held up to her lips gave me a trombone in the pants. Her t-shirt said 'Don't Even Go There'. There was just one place I wanted to go.

Leo and I stayed until the end and I went over to talk to her. She barely spoke English. I said to her that she exuded sensuality on stage. Of course, I meant that she made me so horny that I wanted to lead her to a corner and jazz her right there. Leo translated that into Hungarian for her – the sensuality part, not the horny part. She said she was pleased to hear it. Then we were interrupted by her boyfriend, a bear-like heavy metal guy with a goatee. Needless to say, my bone never got blown.

Leo also took me to one of the famous Turkish baths – a little expensive but totally worth it. We floated around in a large, open-air, heated pool, while a cold wind blew over our heads. An ugly couple fucked in a far corner of the pool. In the shower, men of all ages showered totally naked without a dangling care. I did the same and felt liberated.

On my last day in Budapest, I took the train to Vienna to see Mark. He had organized a loose jam session for me at Celeste with some very interesting musicians. I read poetry with all those guys improvising. It was smokin'. Got back to Budapest the same night and flew to Paris in the morning. The trip helped me lighten up. Back home, I gobbled up the second season of *Californication*. That helped too. Given a choice, I think I'd rather be Hank Moody than Jack Kerouac.

It was through Louise that I met Valentine, a charming girl with a plain face and thick glasses over her myopic eyes. She was some sort of artist. There was something about her that made me want to get to know her better. I called her now and then, and we would go for a drink or for a walk behind the cathedral, along the river. Every time I went out with Valentine, Louise was at work or too tired to go out, or was off to Angers. So it was just Valentine and me. We didn't say much. I complained about the city and we commented on this and that. After one such walk, as we were bidding each other goodbye, I held her hand lightly by the wrist, and she deliberately folded her fingers so they closed on the back of my hand.

I rang her a few weeks later and invited her over to my place to show me something on Photoshop. She came over, looking cute with her short blond hair tied in two tails behind her head, held by elastics with bright red wooden balls. Along with her knee-length denims, it gave her the appearance of a little girl, or an elf, with glasses. When she took off her coat and turned around to put it somewhere, my eyes inevitably turned to her ass. We went to the study to work on the computer. I fiddled with her hairbands while she showed me how to make a logo on Photoshop. I wanted to kiss her to show my gratitude, but stayed put.

Later, as we drank tea in the living room, I put on some hard-boiled swing by the Royal Crown Review. She said, 'Wow, I wouldn't know how to dance to that.'

'C'mon, let's swing,' I replied, and pulled her up and made her swirl, turn and jive. We even did a little slow cheek-to-cheek. I longed to kiss her, but couldn't find the right moment. While we were dancing, facing each other, my thigh rubbed against hers, and I got hard. I think she felt it. After that, she said she had to leave because she didn't want to miss the bus. Nothing in her face showed that she said that out of embarrassment, sounded like it was really about the bus. As we said goodbye and I kissed her on the cheek, she held my hand lightly.

We got together again a few weeks later, and went for a walk in the evening. She looked even cuter than the last time, with the same bright red hair-elastics, loose linen trousers, a long red cotton shirt that came midway down her thigh, a sort of European kurta. We walked down to the cathedral, which looked magnificent in the evening sun with its blue stained glass and fine etchings. I loved going to the cathedral to feel the vibes and soak in its centuries-old grandeur.

The huge door to the cathedral was wide open and the entrance was bathed in sunlight. We went in and walked down the aisle, admiring all the sculptures and commenting on how dirty the walls were, and decided they kept the lights so dim to prevent visitors from seeing the filth. I reckoned it would take a hundred years and all the Templars' money that was spent to build the cathedral, to restore it to its original glory.

I tugged at the confession boxes, hoping to find one open. I always did that, I was curious to know what a confession box here looked like from the inside. You couldn't see anything through the woodwork because there were dark curtains on the inside. So I always checked, in case one was left unlocked by mistake. As I pulled at the confession box after we passed the Black Madonna, it came open. Wow! Adrenaline churned in my balls.

'Hey, I've got to go in,' I whispered to her. She looked confused. There was nobody near us except some tourists in the back, close to the altar, not looking in our direction. I grabbed her hand, opened the door of the confession box, slipped inside and pulled her in. I caught a glimpse of perplexity in her face as the door closed.

There we were, inside the dark confession box, standing very close to each other, my hands on her waist – there was no room to place them anywhere else – my manhood already throbbing with excitement. I was breathing heavily and my heart was beating superfast. It was the thrill of being right next to her in a closed box, the fear of being caught and the ensuing embarrassment. I leaned into her ear and whispered, 'I have a confession to make.'

'Oh, yeah?' she whispered. I kissed her below her ear, she didn't move. I kissed her cheek.

'What are you doing?' she asked. I kissed her neck, then pressed my lips against her mouth gently. She responded with passion, and my grip on her waist tightened as I pulled her closer, feeling her breasts against my chest. I felt like I was in a dream.

And just like in a dream, as I held her ass and pressed her crotch against mine, I came in an uncontrollable rush. All right, that makes me sound more like Charlie Runkle than Hank Moody. But, honestly, this was like in a dream. Can you control getting wet in the middle of a wet dream?

'Ooh la la,' I whispered.

'Ooh la la,' she whispered back. Obviously, despite the dark, she realized what had just happened. We stayed like that for a few seconds.

'Let's get out of here,' I said.

I opened the door and we got out. Outside the cathedral, we smiled sheepishly and I said I had to go home. I could have asked her to come along but didn't. Uncharacteristically, I was a little embarrassed. She said okay. I said I would be in touch, and took the shortest possible route home.

I called her the next day to ask if she wanted to go for a free jazz gig in Paris on Saturday. Some musicians I knew were playing at La Gallerie. She said yes. On Saturday, we met near the Bastille a few hours before the concert. I gave her two quick pecks on the cheek and a longer one on the mouth. We walked around, our hands touching. She tried to talk about what we were doing. She reminded me that I was married.

'I like you and you like me and we're here. Let's just savour this moment and be happy now. We can talk about the rest later. Let's live in the now,' I told her. I think she understood.

We were at the venue at about eight-thirty. I introduced Valentine to the musicians. They were sipping wine, still waiting for people to turn up. I took the opportunity to show her the basement of La Gallerie. Sometimes the gigs took place down there, though not that night. We went down the narrow wooden staircase and I flipped on the light. It was a spacious basement with a little bandstand on one end and a tiny bar on the other. In between, there were cushioned benches. As she was looking around, I put my hands around her waist from behind, and reached out to cup her breasts. She turned her head to one side and our lips met in a kiss. Upstairs, the saxophone began to scream and the piano began to pling. I sat down on a bench and had her sit astride me. That night, free jazz and free love came together. We remained there until the music stopped and people began to clap.

We didn't see each other after that. It was an amazing night but not something that could be repeated. I fantasized about her for many months.

That summer, Louise and I went to the French Riviera, *la Côte d'Azure*, and stayed on a grassroots campsite in the little village of La Colle sur Loup. We went to the beaches, packed with tanned skin and bare breasts, and strolled through the narrow streets among colourful buildings in Nice, Cannes, Antibes and Grasse.

Louise drove us through dangerously winding hills to the wonderful medieval villages of St Paul de Vence, Gourdon and La Tourette. In the air-conditioned car, we hummed along to Blossom Dearie's '*Plus je t'embrasse*' on the radio. We stopped at the markets and bought the local specialities – dried tomatoes, tapenade, olives, bread, roast chicken. We ate on a bench in a public square or in a park and drank from the water fountains. In St Paul de Vence, we attended the village ball and danced away to '*Ca m'énèreve*'.

It's a bundle of very pleasant memories, and this time we didn't fight. Louise had planned the trip, as usual. I would never experience so many things if it weren't for her. She knows all the cool places. She is the best of the best things that have happened to me in the past ten years.

When we first talked about marriage, I knew I was trading my freedom for survival. That as a married man I would be tied to one woman and wouldn't be able to fuck around. But I have been very lucky to have found Louise. She is the kind of girl that's made of love and for love. And she's put up with my tantrums, mood swings, inconsistencies and everything that's negative and dark in me. And there's a lot of that, as you can probably tell by now. She has provided me with the comfort of what you call home – with food, love, companionship and a lot of laughter – and she made possible my total integration with this culture. Every day, I learn something new from her. If it weren't for her, I would never have heard of Nijinsky or Béjart, nor watched *Jules et Jim*. She understands my failings, she knows my fears and my strengths. She takes me in her arms and says things like, 'No, you're not a failure. You came to France and chose to pursue music and culture, not the easiest of paths. Most people get to indulge in their passions only later in life and you have done that in the prime of your youth. For better or worse, it's in your nature to have a life that's different from that of others. And if you're not happy with what you do, you always find a way to do something about it… And don't forget, I love you *beaucoup*, *beaucoup*, and I'm with you in whatever you do.'

Our love has grown over the years, our relationship has evolved. There have been fights, tears, shouting, hitting, and more recently, serious thoughts of divorce. But we're still together. Yes, I have been cruel and selfish, I fucked around because I didn't want to fight my natural urges. But our trip to the French Riviera did something to me. I decided that my wife deserved from me the same undivided, unconditional love she reserved for me. I decided to be strong and not to jump at the first available opportunity to let my pants down.

You know, when people ask me why I came to France, I usually say something smart-alec like, 'Because they told me that French women were really hot.' Or, 'For wine, women and jazz.'

Well, my lust for blue-eyed blondes with beauteous behinds certainly was a big reason. But the greatest reason of all was that I wanted to get away from the million little things that were driving me crazy in India. I always felt like a square peg in a round hole there. Just like some people have this feeling of being a woman trapped inside a man's body, I felt trapped in the wrong kind of environment. I wanted to go some place where I could feel free.

In the land of Camus, Sartre and Alain Delon, I felt at home from the very first day. Like a fish in water. This is where I was meant to be. I'm not saying everything about France is perfect, but it's an environment where I felt like I was growing, where I had access to things, where I connected. Home isn't about living in your motherland but about living in an environment that is conducive to the well-being of your mind. Where you can feel the rapture of being alive.

Sure, I'm glad about the arty things I've done. True, I took the road less travelled. My gripe with life is that I haven't gone very far down that road. I haven't been able to carve a place for myself. All this moaning must sound absurd to you intelligent folks out there. You'd say everyone has a choice, everyone can do something to change their life, right? Well, you gotta walk in my shoes to know where it hurts. My problem is that I don't even know what I want. There was a time when I thought I wanted to promote jazz. Then I wanted to be a performing poet myself. But reading aloud other people's old poetry does not a poet make. Besides, being a performer was just as hard as being a promoter. I could earn a steadier income by teaching English. But I couldn't even find a respectable permanent teaching job and I'm not sure I would even enjoy it for long if I did find one. And I have no more ideas. The social club idea was a good one but it didn't work because it was based on the fallacious notion that I like people. But the truth is, the only people I like are me, myself and I. I am thirty-two and life is quicksand, slowly and steadily sucking me in.

The world is full of people who succeed despite lack of education, lack of money, even lack of a limb and other serious limiting factors. How do they do it? I don't think it's want of qualifications or resources that's holding me back. I think it's just me and my kismet.

Bad kismet gives you a life that sucks. Good kismet results in happy events and serendipitous coincidences. It was a stroke of pure good kismet that I came to France and found Louise, and jazz. But in order to lead a successful life, kismet's got to be in your favour every step of the way. With a half-assed kismet like mine, you'll most likely be stuck with a half-baked success. Like it's happening to me now – after my initial good luck, stagnation. Growing up in India, I always heard that you bring to earth your own kismet, meaning that one's kismet is pre-defined. Good or bad, you can't do much to alter it. I buy that idea as well. I know it's the twenty-first century but I still buy it. Call me a frustrated fool. My own spin on it is that one's life is like a jazz standard, where the theme and the arrangement are already written out, with scope for improvisation in the middle. And you are a performer, led by the hand of some invisible composer-conductor. All the striving and the hard work you do in life is part of the improvisation that you indulge in to fill in the time until you get to the out chorus. All the crap that you hear about people making their own destiny and about life being shaped by the choices you make, that's bullshit. You don't make or shape anything. All you do is play out what has already been written out for you. The rags-to-riches stories, they're all written out before they begin. Life is a fixed fight. And it looks like I am about to be knocked out.

The sweet bird of youth is flying me by. Each day brings with it a new strand of grey hair on the sides of my ears. The bald patch on the top of my head is expanding fast. At twenty, I liked to imagine that by thirty I'd be rich and famous. That never happened. Of course there are stories of late bloomers to reckon with, you know, young losers turned old winners. For instance, David Ogilvy got his first advertising job at thirty-five. Henry Miller was unpublished at forty-two. Humphrey Bogart tasted success only after forty. I get no consolation in their stories. I am aware of my own mediocrity.

It won't be any good if kismet takes a shine on me when I'm old and unfuckable. In common human experience, the Lord taketh with one hand and giveth with the other. Generally, people lacking in one area are strong in another. Like those with no brawn have brains and those with no brains have brawn. Seems like in my case the Lord forgot the balancing act. He didn't bother to compensate my smallness and average looks with brains or money or seductive charm or charisma. Or a super-sized dick. Everything in this small package is small, and condemned to a small life. Did I cross the oceans to the land of my dreams just to be a nobody? Just a brick in the wall?

What a waste.

Voilà! There goes my entire Ramayana, the zero's journey. It's December already. Ten years since I first came to France. Louise hates her job. I hate myself. Dad is having a puja performed for me in India. It's meant to align my stars, please the gods and straighten things out. My brother says it worked for him when he needed divine intervention and that I should be cool and believe in it.

I'll believe in anything, bro. I'll kiss God's ass and not only sell my soul to the devil but suck his cock too, if only I could put things right in this life, from this moment on.

2010

Epilogue

Life changed this year.

In January, I got myself a few teaching hours at St Peter's Institute and started staying in Angers four days a week at my in-laws' house. I loved being able to spend more time in Angers and if I had one more contract, I'd stay in Angers the entire week. I realized that I wanted to move back as soon as possible.

Louise got more and more fed up with her job. Her organization had a new director who made Louise very unhappy, so much so that she got depressed and stayed home on a very long sick leave.

In March, I got myself an interview with the head of English at ESMA, the prestigious business school in Angers. I had once met Lawrence Boyd, the head, at Pam and David's ten years ago and in the intervening years he had seen my picture in the newspaper a couple of times in connection with jazz events, so he remembered me. We had a nice chat, he asked me how I'd explain 'present perfect' and how I'd deal with discipline issues in a class of twenty rich kids. I answered all his questions with confidence and Lawrence put me down for a substantial number of hours starting September. Just like that. I hadn't gone there thinking it would be so easy. I wished I had got in touch with him earlier. Louise was proud of me for finally getting off my ass and doing something. Then I sent out my CV to a bunch of other schools and university departments. A number of people got back to me asking about my availability.

Louise and I had a talk and she agreed that I had more of a future in Angers and that if I moved back she would too. She couldn't stand going back to her job and was entirely disenchanted with the whole milieu of dance and culture where jobs were hard to find and didn't pay very well either. 'I'd rather teach philosophy,' she said. I thought that was a cool idea. We decided not only to move back to Angers but to buy an apartment of our own.

Over the next two months, we visited about ten apartments before we found the one. It was on the first floor of a 1950s' building that used to be a big family home and was now divided into three apartments, one on each floor. We loved the wooden floor and the natural light in the apartment and imagined doing it up with vintage furniture from second-hand shops. I was already visualizing a *Mad Men*-style decor.

I negotiated a good price, though I think I could have done better had I bargained harder. After the usual running around, getting a loan and paperwork sorted out, we finally signed the settlement and moved into our new home. Louise's parents and grandparents helped us make the down payment.

After the move, Louise started teaching philosophy at a high school and I at four different schools. Louise liked her new job, I loved mine. More work, more money, more excitement. I couldn't help wonder why this hadn't happened sooner. Why didn't I seek out these opportunities on my own? Why didn't I send my CV out to all those people every semester? Why did I focus so much on jazz and starting a business instead of looking for more work? I got to thinking all this, regretting what I did or did not do in the past and what I did not have but could have had if I had done this or that...

STOP!

... a voice in my head told me, stop, and don't fuck this up. Who knows why things did or didn't happen in the past? Everything happens in its own time. Maybe in the past the time was not right. The time is right now. Kismet is being kind to me now. I have a good life, a wonderful wife, an apartment to my name in this beautiful part of the world.

And I just met Camille, the girl with the reddest hair and the hottest ass in town.

Thanks

Pierre Astier, for believing in my work and sticking with it.

Neelini Sarkar, for picking it up and making it publishable.

HarperCollins India, for publishing it.

Writer Stephen Clarke, for useful advice and help.

Alok M, Jean A, Julien D, Pat E, Paul W, Jolyon D and Rupert M, for being a friend in need.

Laurence H, for good ideas.

Vivek, for being a good brother.

Special thanks to Patrick and Martine, and Robert and Annette, for accepting me in their family.

Jack Kerouac, Henry Miller, J D Salinger and Langston Hughes, for inspiration.